Salthaven by W.W. Jacobs

William Wymark Jacobs was born on September 8th, 1863 in the Wapping district of London, England. Jacobs grew up near the docks, where his father was a wharf manager. The docks and river side would be a constant theme of his writing in years to come.

Although surrounded by poverty, he received a formal education in London, first at a private prep school and later at the Birkbeck Literary and Scientific Institute.

His working life began with a less than exciting clerical position at the Post Office Savings Bank. Jacobs put his imagination to good use writing short stories, sketches and articles, many for the Post Office house publication "Blackfriars Magazine."

In 1896 Jacobs published Many Cargoes, a selection of sea-faring yarns, which established him as a popular writer with a knack for authentic dialogue and trick endings.

A year later he published a novelette, The Skipper's Wooing, and in 1898 another collection of short stories; Sea Urchins. These works painted vivid pictures of dockland and seafaring London full of colourful characters.

By 1899, Jacobs was able to quit the post office and write full-time.

He married the noted suffragist Agnes Eleanor Williams (who had been jailed for her protest activities) in 1900. They set up households both in Loughton, Essex and in central London.

The publication in 1902 of At Sunwich Port and Dialstone Lane, in 1904, cemented Jacobs' reputation as one of the leading British authors of the new century.

There followed a string of further successful publications, including Captain's All (1905), Night Watches (1914), The Castaways (1916), and Sea Whispers (1926).

Though Jacobs would create little in the way of new work after 1911, he still wrote and was recognized as a leading humorist, ranked alongside such writers as P. G. Wodehouse.

William Wymark Jacobs died in a North London nursing home in Hornsey Lane, Islington on September 1st, 1943.

Index of Contents

CHAPTER I

Mr. John Vyner, ship-owner, pushed his chair back from his writing-table and gazed with kindly condescension at the chief clerk as he stood before it with a handful of papers.

"We shall be able to relieve you of some of your work soon, Hartley," he said, slowly. "Mr. Robert will come into the firm next week." The chief clerk bowed.

"Three years at Cambridge," resumed Mr. Vyner, meditatively, "and two years spent up and down the world studying the business methods of other nations ought to render him invaluable to us."

"No doubt, sir," said Hartley. "It is an excellent training."

"For a time," said the ship-owner, leaning back and placing the tips of his fingers together, "for a time I am afraid that he will have to have your room. Later on—ha—if a room should—ha—fall vacant in the building, we might consider taking it."

"Yes, sir," said the other.

"And, of course," resumed Mr. Vyner, "there is one great advantage in your being in the general office which must not be overlooked; you can keep an eye on the juniors better."

"It is cheerful, too, sir," suggested the chief clerk; "the only thing—"

"Yes?" said Mr. Vyner, somewhat loudly.

Mr. Hartley shrank a little. "I was going to say that it is rather a small room for Mr. Robert," he said, quickly.

"It will do for a time," said the other.

"And—and I think I told you, sir, that there is an unpleasant sm—odour."

Mr. Vyner knitted his brows. "I offered to have that seen to, but you said that you didn't mind it," he remarked.

"Just so, sir," said Hartley; "but I was thinking of Mr. Robert. He might not like it; it's very strong at times—very strong indeed."

"You ought to have had it attended to before," said Mr. Vyner, with some severity. "You had better call at Gillows' on your way home and ask them to send a man up first thing to-morrow morning."

He drew his chair to the table again, and Hartley, after lingering a moment, withdrew to his own room.

Ten out of his thirty-five years of service had been passed there, and he stifled a sigh as he looked at the neat array of drawers and pigeon-holes, the window overlooking the bridge and harbour, and the stationer's almanac which hung over the fireplace. The japanned letter-rack and the gum-bottle on the small mantelpiece were old friends.

The day's work completed, he walked home in sober thought. It was a pleasant afternoon in May, but he was too preoccupied to pay any heed to the weather, and, after informing a man who stopped him to tell him that he had lost a wife, six children, and a right leg, that it was just five minutes past six, resumed his way with a hazy idea of having been useful to a fellow-creature.

He brightened a little as he left the bustle of the town behind, and from sheer force of habit glanced at the trim front-gardens as he passed. The cloud lifted still more as he reached his own garden and mentally compared his flowers with those he had just passed.

His daughter was out, and tea for one was laid in the front room. He drew his chair to the table, and taking up the tea-pot, which the maid had just brought in, poured himself out a cup of tea.

He looked round the comfortable room with pleasure. After all, nobody could take that from him. He stirred his tea and had just raised the cup to his lips when he set it down untasted and sat staring blankly before him. A low rumble of voices from the kitchen fell unpleasantly on his ear; and his daughter Joan had left instructions too specific to be misunderstood as to his behaviour in the event of Rosa entertaining male company during her absence. He coughed twice, loudly, and was glad to note the disappearance of the rumble. Pleased with his success he coughed a third time, a sonorous cough charged with importance. A whispered rumble, possibly a suggestion of withdrawal, came from the kitchen.

"Only his tea gone the wrong way," he heard, reassuringly, from Rosa.

The rumble, thus encouraged, deepened again. It became confident and was heard to laugh. Mr. Hartley rose and, standing on the hearthrug with legs apart, resolved to play the man. He leaned over and rang the bell. The voices stopped. Then he heard Rosa say, "Not him! you stay where you are."

She came slowly in response to the bell, and thrusting a yellow head in at the door gazed at him inquiringly.

"I—I want a little more hot water," said her master, mildly.

"More?" repeated Rosa. "Why, I brought you over a pint."

"I want some more," said Mr. Hartley. Then a bright thought struck him. "I am expecting Miss Joan home every minute," he added, significantly.

Rosa tossed her head. "She ain't coming home till nine," she remarked, "so if it's only for her you want the hot water, you won't want it."

"I—I thought I heard a man's voice," he said at last.

"Very good," said her master, with an attempt at dignity; "you can go."

Rosa went, whistling. Mr. Hartley, feeling that he had done all that could be expected of a man, sat down and resumed his tea. The rumbling from the kitchen, as though in an endeavour to make up for lost time, became continuous. It also became louder and more hilarious. Pale and determined Mr. Hartley rose a second time and, seizing the bell-pull, rang violently.

"Does anybody want to see me?" he inquired, as Rosa's head appeared.

"You? No," was the reply.

"I thought," said her master, gazing steadily at the window, "I thought somebody was inquiring for me."

"Well, there hasn't been," said Rosa.

Mr. Hartley, with a magisterial knitting of the brows, which had occasionally been found effective with junior clerks, affected to ponder.

"I—I thought I heard a man's voice," he said at last.

"Nobody's been inquiring for you," said Rosa calmly. "If they did I should come in and let you know. Nobody's been for you that I've heard of, and I don't see how they could come without me knowing it."

"Just so," said Mr. Hartley. "Just so."

He turned to the mantelpiece for his tobacco-jar, and Rosa, after standing for some time at the "ready" with a hostile stare, cleared her throat noisily and withdrew. The voices in the kitchen broke out with renewed vehemence; Mr. Hartley coughed again—a cough lacking in spirit—and, going out at the front door, passed through the side-entrance to the garden and tended his plants with his back to the kitchen window.

Hard at work at the healthful pastime of weeding, his troubles slipped from him. The path became littered with little tufts of grass, and he Was just considering the possibility of outflanking the birch-broom, which had taken up an advantageous position by the kitchen window, when a young man came down the side-entrance and greeted him with respectful enthusiasm.

"I brought you these," he said, opening a brown leather bag and extracting a few dried roots. "I saw an advertisement. I forget the name of them, but they have beautiful trumpet-shaped flowers. They are free growers, and grow yards and yards the first year."

"And miles and miles the second," said Mr. Hartley, regarding them with extraordinary ferocity. "Bindweed is the name, and once get it in your garden and you'll never get rid of it."

"That wasn't the name in the advertisement," said the other, dubiously.

"I don't suppose it was," said Hartley. "You've got a lot to learn in gardening yet, Saunders."

"Yes, sir," said the other; "I've got a good teacher, though."

Mr. Hartley almost blushed. "And how is your garden getting on?" he inquired.

"It's—it's getting on," said Mr. Saunders, vaguely.

"I must come and have a look at it," said Hartley.

"Not yet," said the young man, hastily. "Not yet. I shouldn't like you to see it just yet. Is Miss Hartley well?"

Mr. Hartley said she was, and, in an abstracted fashion, led the way down the garden to where an enormous patch of land—or so it seemed to Mr. Saunders—awaited digging. The latter removed his coat and, hanging it with great care on an apple tree, turned back his cuffs and seized the fork.

"It's grand exercise," said Mr. Hartley, after watching him for some time.

"Grand," said Mr. Saunders, briefly.

"As a young man I couldn't dig enough," continued the other, "but nowadays it gives me a crick in the back."

"Always?" inquired Mr. Saunders, with a slight huskiness.

"Always," said Mr. Hartley. "But I never do it now; Joan won't let me."

Mr. Saunders sighed at the name and resumed his digging. "Miss Hartley out?" he asked presently, in a casual voice.

"Yes; she won't be home till late," said the other. "We can have a fine evening's work free of interruptions. I'll go and get on with my weeding."

He moved off and resumed his task; Mr. Saunders, with a suppressed groan, went on with his digging. The ground got harder and harder and his back seemed almost at breaking-point. At intervals he had what gardeners term a "straight-up," and with his face turned toward the house listened intently for any sounds that might indicate the return of its mistress.

"Half-past eight," said Hartley at last; "time to knock off. I've put a few small plants in your bag for you; better put them in in the morning before you start off."

Mr. Saunders thanked him, and reaching down his coat put it on and followed Mr. Hartley to the house. The latter, steering him round by the side-entrance, accompanied him to the front gate.

"If you would like to borrow my roller or lawn-mower at any time," he said, cordially, "I should be very pleased to lend them to you. It isn't very far."

Mr. Saunders, who would sooner have died than have been seen dragging a roller through the streets, thanked him warmly. With an idea of prolonging his stay, he suggested looking at them.

"They're locked up now," said Mr. Hartley. "See them another time. Good-night."

"Good-night," said Mr. Saunders. "I'll look in to-morrow evening, if I may."

"No use to-morrow," Mr. Hartley called after him; "there will be nobody at home but Joan."

CHAPTER II

Mr. Robert VYNER entered upon his new duties with enthusiasm. The second day he was at the office half an hour before anybody else; on the third day the staff competed among themselves for the honour of arriving first, and greeted him as respectfully as their feelings would permit when he strolled in at a quarter to eleven. The arrival of the senior partner on the day following at a phenomenally early hour, for the sake of setting an example to the junior, filled them with despair. Their spirits did not revive until Mr. John had given up the task as inconvenient and useless.

A slight fillip was given to Robert's waning enthusiasm by the arrival of new furniture for his room. A large mahogany writing-table, full of drawers and pigeon-holes, gave him a pleasant sense of importance, and the revolving chair which went with it afforded a welcome relief to a young and ardent nature. Twice the office-boy had caught the junior partner, with his legs tucked up to avoid collisions, whirling wildly around, and had waited respectfully at the door for the conclusion of the performance.

"It goes a bit stiff, Bassett," said the junior partner.

"Yessir," said Bassett.

"I'm trying to ease it a bit," explained Mr. Robert.

"Yessir," said Bassett again.

Mr. Robert regarded him closely. An undersized boy in spectacles, with a large head and an air of gravity and old age on his young features, which the junior thought somewhat ill-placed for such an occasion.

"I suppose you never twizzle round on your chair, Bassett?" he said, slowly.

Bassett shivered at the idea. "No, sir," he said, solemnly; "I've got my work to do."

Mr. Robert sought for other explanations. "And, of course, you have a stool," he remarked; "you couldn't swing round on that."

"Not even if I wanted to, sir," said the unbending Bassett.

Mr. Robert nodded, and taking some papers from his table held them before his face and surveyed the youth over the top. Bassett stood patiently to attention.

"That's all right," said the other; "thank you."

"Thank you, sir," said Bassett, turning to the door.

"By the way," said Mr. Robert, eying him curiously as he turned the handle, "what exercise do you take?"

"Exercise, sir?" said Bassett.

Mr. Robert nodded. "What do you do of an evening for amusement after the arduous toils of the day are past? Marbles?"

"No, sir," said the outraged one. "If I have any time to spare I amuse myself with a little shorthand."

"Amuse!" exclaimed the other. He threw himself back in his chair and, sternly checking its inclination to twirl again, sought for a flaw in the armour of this paragon. "And what else do you do in the way of recreation?"

"I've got a vivarium, sir."

Mr. Robert hesitated, but curiosity got the better of his dignity. "What's that?" he inquired.

"A thing I keep frogs and toads in, sir," was the reply.

Mr. Robert, staring hard at him, did his honest best to check the next question, but it came despite himself. "Are you—are you married, Bassett?" he inquired.

Bassett regarded him calmly. "No, sir," he said, with perfect gravity. "I live at home with my mother."

The junior partner gave him a nod of dismissal, and for some time sat gazing round the somewhat severely furnished office, wondering with some uneasiness what effect such surroundings might have on a noble but impressionable temperament. He brought round a few sketches the next day to brighten the walls, and replated the gum-bottle and other useful ornaments by some German beer-mugs.

Even with these aids to industry he found the confinement of office somewhat irksome, and, taking a broad view of his duties, gradually relieved Bassett of his errands to the docks. It was necessary, he told himself, to get a thorough grasp of the whole business of ship-owning. In the stokeholds of Vyner and Son's' steamships he talked learnedly on coal with the firemen, and, quite unaided, hit on several schemes for the saving of coal—all admirable except for the fact: that several knots per hour would be lost.

"The thing is to take an all-round view," he said to Captain. Trimblett, of the SS. Indian Chief, as he strolled back with that elderly mariner from the ship to the office one day.

"That's it, sir," said the captain.

"Don't waste, and, at the same time, don't pinch," continued Mr. Robert, oracularly.

"That's business in a nutshell," commented the captain. "Don't spoil the ship for a ha'porth of tar, and, on the other hand, don't get leaving the tar about for other people to sit on."

"But you got it off," said Robert, flushing. "You told me you had."

"As far as tar ever can be got off," asserted the captain, gloomily. "Yes. Why I put my best trousers on this morning," he continued, in a tone of vague wonder, "I'm sure I don't know. It was meant to be, I suppose; it's all for some wise purpose: that we don't know of."

"Wise fiddlesticks!" exclaimed Robert, shortly—"Your particular brand of fatalism is the most extraordinary nonsense I ever heard of. What it means: is that thousands of years ago, or millions, perhaps, was decided that I should be born on purpose to tar your blessed trousers."

"That and other things," said the immovable captain. "It's all laid down for us, everything we do, and we can't help doing it. When I put on those trousers this morning—"

"Oh, hang your trousers," said Robert. "You said it didn't matter, and you've been talking about nothing else ever since."

"I won't say another word about it," said the captain. "I remember the last pair I had done; a pair o' white ducks. My steward it was; one o' those silly, fat-headed, staring-eyed, garping—"

"Go on," said the other, grimly.

"Nice, bright young fellows," concluded the captain, hastily; "he got on very well, I believe."

"After he left you, I suppose?" said Mr. Vyner, smoothly.

"Yes," said the innocent captain. He caught a glance of the other's face and ruminated. "After I had broken him of his silly habits," he added.

He walked along smiling, and, raising his cap with a flourish, beamed in a fatherly manner on a girl who was just passing. Robert replaced his hat and glanced over his left shoulder.

"Who is that?" he inquired. "I saw her the other day; her face seems familiar to me."

"Joan Hartley," replied the captain. "Nathaniel Hartley's daughter. To my mind, the best and prettiest girl in Salthaven."

"Eh?" said the other, staring. "Hartley's daughter? Why, I should have thought—"

The best and prettiest girl in Salthaven

"Yes, sir?" said Captain Trimblett, after a pause.

"Nothing," concluded Robert, lamely. "She doesn't look like it; that's all."

"She's got his nose," maintained the captain, with the obstinate air of a man prepared to go to the stake for his opinions. "Like as two peas their noses are; you'd know them for father and daughter anywhere by that alone."

Mr. Vyner assented absently. He was wondering where the daughter of the chief clerk got her high looks from.

"Very clever girl," continued the captain. "She got a scholarship and went to college, and then, when her poor mother died, Hartley was so lonely that she gave it all up and came home to keep house for him."

"Quite a blue-stocking," suggested Robert.

"There's nothing of the blue-stocking about her," said the captain, warmly. "In fact, I shouldn't be surprised if she became engaged soon."

Mr. Vyner became interested. "Oh!" he said, with an instinctive glance over his left shoulder.

Captain Trimblett nodded sagely. "Young fellow of the name of Saunders," he said slowly.

"Oh!" said the other again.

"You might have seen him at Wilson's, the ship-broker's," pursued the captain. "Bert Saunders his name is. Rather a dressy youngster, perhaps. Generally wears a pink shirt and a very high stand-up collar—one o' those collars that you have to get used to."

Mr. Vyner nodded.

"He's not good enough for her," said the captain, shaking his head. "But then, nobody is. Looked at that way it's all right."

"You seem to take a great interest in it," said Robert.

"He came to me with his troubles," said Captain Trimblett, bunching up his gray beard in his hand reflectively. "Leastways, he made a remark or two which I took up. Acting under my advice he is taking up gardening."

Mr. Vyner glanced at him in mystification.

"Hartley is a great gardener," explained the other with a satisfied smile. "What is the result? He can go there when he likes, so to speak. No awkwardness or anything of that sort. He can turn up there bold as brass to borrow a trowel, and take three or four hours doing it."

"You're a danger to society," said Robert, shaking his head.

"People ought to marry while they're young," said the captain. "If they don't, like as not they're crazy to marry in their old age. There's my landlord here at Tranquil Vale, fifty-two next birthday, and over his ears in love. He has got it about as bad as a man can have it."

"And the lady?" inquired Robert.

"She's all right," said the captain. He lowered his voice confidentially. "It's Peter's sister, that's the trouble. He's afraid to let her know. All we can do is to drop a little hint here and a little hint there, so as to prepare her for the news when it's broken to her."

"Is she married?" inquired Robert, pausing as they reached the office.

"No," said Captain Trimblett; "widow."

Mr. Vyner gave a low whistle. "When do you sail, cap'n?" he inquired, in a voice oily with solicitude.

"Soon as my engine-room repairs are finished, I suppose," said the other, staring.

"And you—you are giving her hints about courtship and marriage?" inquired Mr. Vyner, in tones of carefully-modulated surprise.

"She's a sensible woman," said the captain, reddening, "and she's no more likely to marry again than I am."

"Just what I was thinking," said Mr. Vyner.

He shook his head, and, apparently deep in thought, turned and walked slowly up the stairs. He was pleased to notice as he reached the first landing that the captain was still standing where he had left him, staring up the stairs.

CHAPTER III

In a somewhat ruffled state of mind Captain Trimblett pursued his way toward Tranquil Vale, a. row of neat cottages situated about a mile and a half from the town, and inhabited principally by retired mariners. The gardens, which ran down to the river, boasted a particularly fine strain of flag-staffs; battered figure-heads in swan-like attitudes lent a pleasing touch of colour, and old boats sawn in halves made convenient arbours in which to sit and watch the passing pageant of the sea.

At No. 5 the captain paused to pass a perfectly dry boot over a scraper of huge dimensions which guarded the entrance, and, opening the door, finished off on the mat. Mrs. Susanna Chinnery, who was setting tea, looked up at his entrance, and then looked at the clock.

"Kettle's just on the boil," she remarked.

"Your kettle always is," said the captain, taking a chair—"when it's time for it to be, I mean," he added, hastily, as Mrs. Chinnery showed signs of correcting him.

"It's as easy to be punctual as otherwise," said Mrs. Chinnery; "easier, if people did but know it."

"So it is," murmured the captain, and sat gazing, with a sudden wooden expression, at a picture opposite of the eruption of Vesuvius.

"Peter's late again," said Mrs. Chinnery, in tones of hopeless resignation.

"Business, perhaps," suggested Captain Trimblett, still intent on Vesuvius.

"For years and years you could have set the clock by him," continued Mrs. Chinnery, bustling out to the kitchen and bustling back again with the kettle; "now I never know when to expect him. He was late yesterday."

Captain Trimblett cleared his throat. "He saw a man nearly run over," he reminded her.

"Yes; but how long would that take him?" retorted Mrs. Chinnery. "If the man had been run over I could have understood it."

The captain murmured something about shock.

"On Friday he was thirty-three minutes late," continued the other.

"Friday," said the faithful captain. "Friday he stopped to listen to a man playing the bagpipes—a Scotchman."

"That was Thursday," said Mrs. Chinnery.

The captain affected to ponder. "So it was," he said, heartily. "What a memory you have got! Of course, Friday he walked back to the office for his pipe."

"Well, we won't wait for him," said Mrs. Chinnery, taking the head of the table and making the tea. "If he can't come in to time he must put up with his tea being cold. That's the way we were brought up."

"A very good way, too," said the captain. He put a radish into his mouth and, munching slowly, fell to gazing at Vesuvius again. It was not until he had passed his cup up for the second time that a short, red-faced man came quickly into the room and, taking a chair from its place against the wall, brought it to the table and took a seat opposite the captain.

"Late again, Peter," said his sister.

"Been listening to a man playing the cornet," said Mr. Truefitt, briefly.

Captain Trimblett, taking the largest radish he could find, pushed it into his mouth and sat gazing at him in consternation. He had used up two musical instruments in less than a week.

"You're getting fond of music in your old age," said Mrs. Chinnery, tartly. "But you always are late nowadays. When it isn't music it's something else. What's come over you lately I can't think."

Mr. Truefitt cleared his throat for speech, and then, thinking better of it, helped himself to some bread and butter and went on with his meal. His eyes met those of Captain Trimblett and then wandered away to the window. The captain sprang into the breach.

"He wants a wife to keep him in order," he said, with a boldness that took Mr. Truefitt's breath away.

"Wife!" exclaimed Mrs. Chinnery. "Peter!"

She put down her cup and laughed—a laugh so free from disquietude that Mr. Truefitt groaned in spirit.

"He'll go off one of these days." said the captain with affected joviality. "You see if he don't."

Mrs. Chinnery laughed again. "He's a born bachelor," she declared. "Why, he'd sooner walk a mile out of his way any day than meet a woman. He's been like it ever since he was a boy. When I was a girl and brought friends of mine home to tea, Peter would sit like a stuffed dummy and never say a word."

"I've known older bachelors than him to get married," said the captain. "I've known 'em down with it as sudden as heart disease. In a way, it is heart disease, I suppose."

"Peter's heart's all right," said Mrs. Chinnery.

"He might drop down any moment," declared the captain.

Mr. Truefitt, painfully conscious of their regards, passed his cup up for some more tea and made a noble effort to appear amused, as the captain cited instance after instance of confirmed bachelors being led to the altar.

"I broke the ice for you to-day," he said, as they sat after tea in the little summer-house at the bottom of the garden, smoking.

Mr. Truefitt's gaze wandered across the river. "Yes," he said, slowly, "yes."

"I was surprised at myself," said the captain.

"I was surprised at you," said Mr. Truefitt, with some energy. "So far as I can see, you made it worse."

The captain started. "I did it for the best, my lad," he said, reproachfully. "She has got to know some day. You can't be made late by cornets and bagpipes every day."

Mr. Truefitt rumpled his short gray hair. "You see, I promised her," he said, suddenly.

"I know," said the captain, nodding. "And now you've promised Miss Willett."

"When they brought him home dead," said Mr. Truefitt, blowing out a cloud of smoke, "she was just twenty-five. Pretty she was then, cap'n, as pretty a maid as you'd wish to see. As long as I live, Susanna, and have a home, you shall share it'; that's what I said to her."

The captain nodded again.

"And she's kept house for me for twenty-five years," continued Mr. Truefitt; "and the surprising thing to me is the way the years have gone. I didn't realize it until I found an old photograph of hers the other day taken when she was twenty. Men don't change much."

The captain looked at him—at the close-clipped gray whiskers, the bluish lips, and the wrinkles round the eyes. "No," he said, stoutly. "But she could live with you just the same."

The other shook his head. "Susanna would never stand another woman in the house," he said, slowly. "She would go out and earn her own living; that's her pride. And she wouldn't take anything from me. It's turning her out of house and home."

"She'd be turning herself out," said the captain.

"Of course, there is the chance she might marry again," said the other, slowly. "She's had several chances, but she refused 'em all."

"From what she said one day," said the captain, "I got the idea that she has kept from marrying all these years for your sake."

Mr. Truefitt put his pipe down on the table and stared blankly before him. "That's the worst of it," he said, forlornly; "but something will have to be done. I've been engaged three weeks now, and every time I spend a few minutes with Cecilia—Miss Willett—I have to tell a lie about it."

"You do it very well," said his friend. "Very well indeed."

"And Susanna regards me as the most truthful man that ever breathed," continued Mr. Truefitt.

"You've got a truthful look about you," said the captain. "If I didn't know you so well I should have thought the same."

Unconscious of Mr. Truefitt's regards he rose and, leaning his arm on the fence at the bottom of the garden, watched the river.

"Miss Willett thinks she might marry again," said Mr. Truefitt, picking up his pipe and joining him. "She'd make an excellent wife for anybody—anybody."

The captain assented with a nod.

"Nobody could have a better wife," said Mr. Truefitt.

The captain, who was watching an outward-bound barque, nodded again, absently.

"She's affectionate," pursued Mr. Truefitt, "a wonderful housekeeper, a good conversationalist, a good cook, always punctual, always at home, always—"

The captain, surprised at a fluency so unusual, turned and eyed him in surprise. Mr. Truefitt broke off abruptly, and, somewhat red in the face, expressed his fear that the barque would take the mud if she were not careful. Captain Trimblett agreed and, to his friend's relief, turned his back on him to watch her more closely. It was a comfortable position, with his arms on the fence, and he retained it until Mr. Truefitt had returned to the summer-house.

CHAPTER IV

Mr. Robert VYNER had been busy all the afternoon, and the clock still indicated fifteen minutes short of the time at which he had intended to leave. He leaned back in his chair, and, yielding to the slight rotatory movement of that active piece of furniture, indulged in the first twirl for three days. Bassett or no Bassett, it was exhilarating, and, having gone to the limit in one direction, he obtained impetus by a clutch at the table and whirled back again. A smothered exclamation from the door arrested his attention, and putting on the break with some suddenness he found himself looking into the pretty, astonished eyes of Joan Hartley.

"I beg your pardon," she said, in confusion. "I thought it was my father."

"It—it got stuck," said Mr. Vyner, springing up and regarding the chair with great disfavour. "I was trying to loosen it. I shall have to send it back, I'm afraid; it's badly made. There's no cabinet-making nowadays."

Miss Hartley retreated to the doorway.

"I am sorry; I expected to find my father here," she said. "It used to be his room."

"Yes, it was his room," said the young man. "If you will come in and sit down I will send for him."

"It doesn't matter, thank you," said Joan, still standing by the door. "If you will tell me where his room is now, I will go to him."

"He—he is in the general office," said Robert Vyner, slowly.

Miss Hartley bit her lip and her eyes grew sombre.

"Don't go," said Mr. Vyner, eagerly. "I'll go and fetch him. He is expecting you."

"Expecting me?" said the girl. "Why, he didn't know I was coming."

"Perhaps I misunderstood him," murmured Mr. Vyner. "Pressure of business," he said, vaguely, indicating a pile of papers on his table. "Hardly know what people do say to me."

He pushed a comfortable easy-chair to the window, and the girl, after a moment's hesitation, seated herself and became interested in the life outside. Robert Vyner, resuming his seat, leaned back and gazed at her in frank admiration.

"Nice view down the harbour, isn't it?" he said, after a long pause.

Miss Hartley agreed—and sat admiring it.

"Salthaven is a pretty place altogether, I think," continued Robert. "I was quite glad to come back to it. I like the town and I like the people. Except for holidays I haven't been in the place since I was ten."

Miss Hartley, feeling that some comment was expected, said, "Indeed!"

"You have lived here all your life, I suppose?" said the persevering Robert.

"Practically," said Miss Hartley.

Mr. Vyner stole a look at her as she sat sideways by the window. Conscience and his visitor's manner told him that he ought to go for her father; personal inclination told him that there was no hurry. For the first time in his experience the office became most desirable place in the world. He wanted to sit still and look at her, and for some time, despite her restlessness, obeyed his inclinations. She turned at last to ask for her father, and in the fraction of a second he was immersed in a bundle of papers. Knitted brows and pursed lips testified to his absorption. He seized a pen and made an endorsement; looked at it with his head on one side and struck it out again.

"My father?" said Miss Hartley, in a small but determined voice.

Mr. Vyner gazed at her in a preoccupied fashion. Suddenly his face changed.

"Good gracious! yes," he said, springing up and going to the door. "How stupid of me!"

He stepped into the corridor and stood reflecting. In some circumstances he could be business-like enough. After reflecting for three minutes he came back into the room.

"He will be in soon," he said, resuming his seat. Inwardly he resolved to go and fetch him later on— when the conversation flagged, for instance. Meantime he took up his papers and shook his head over them.

"I wish I had got your father's head for business," he said, ruefully.

Miss Hartley turned on him a face from which all primness had vanished. The corners of her mouth broke and her eyes grew soft. She smiled at Mr. Vyner, and Mr. Vyner, pluming himself upon his address, smiled back.

"If I knew half as much as he does," he continued, "I'd—I'd—"

Miss Hartley waited, her eyes bright with expectation.

"I'd," repeated Mr. Vyner, who had rashly embarked on a sentence before he had seen the end of it, "have a jolly easy time of it," he concluded, breathlessly.

Miss Hartley surveyed him in pained surprise. "I thought my father worked very hard," she said, with a little reproach in her voice.

"So he does," said the young man, hastily, "but he wouldn't if he only had my work to do; that's what I meant. As far as he is concerned he works far too hard. He sets an example that is a trouble to all of us except the office-boy. Do you know Bassett?"

Miss Hartley smiled. "My father tells me he is a very good boy," she said.

"A treasure!" said Robert. "'Good' doesn't describe Bassett. He is the sort of boy who would get off a 'bus after paying his fare to kick a piece of orange peel off the pavement. He has been nourished on copy-book headings and 'Sanford and Merton.' Ever read 'Sanford and Merton'?"

"I—I tried to once," said Joan.

"There was no 'trying' with Bassett," said Mr. Vyner, rather severely. "He took to it as a duck takes to water. By modelling his life on its teaching he won a silver medal for never missing an attendance at school."

"Father has seen it," said Joan, with a smile.

"Even the measles failed to stop him," continued Robert. "Day by day, a little more flushed than usual, perhaps, he sat in his accustomed place until the whole school was down with it and had to be closed in consequence. Then, and not till then, did Bassett feel that he had saved the situation."

"I don't suppose he knew it, poor boy," said Joan.

"Anyway, he got the medal," said Robert, "and he has a row of prizes for good conduct. I never had one; not even a little one. I suppose you had a lot?"

Miss Hartley maintained a discreet silence.

"Nobody ever seemed to notice my good conduct," continued Mr. Vyner, still bent on making conversation. "They always seemed to notice the other kind fast enough; but the 'good' seemed to escape them."

He sighed faintly, and glancing at the girl, who was looking out of the window again, took up his pen and signed his blotting-paper.

"I suppose you know the view from that window pretty well?" he said, putting the paper aside with great care.

"Ever since I was a small girl," said Joan, looking round. "I used to come here sometimes and wait for father. Not so much lately; and now, of course—"

Mr. Vyner looked uncomfortable. "I hope you will come to this room whenever you want to see him," he said, earnestly. "He—he seemed to prefer being in the general office."

Miss Hartley busied herself with the window again. "Seemed to prefer," she said, impatiently, under her breath. "Yes."

There was a long silence, which Mr. Vyner, gazing in mute consternation at the vision of indignant prettiness by the window, felt quite unable to break. He felt that the time had at last arrived at which he might safely fetch Mr. Hartley without any self-upbraidings later on, and was just about to rise when the faint tap at the door by which Bassett always justified his entrance stopped him, and Bassett entered the room with some cheques for signature. Despite his habits, the youth started slightly as he saw the visitor, and then, placing the cheques before Mr. Vyner, stood patiently by the table while he signed them.

"That will do," said the latter, as he finished. "Thank you."

"Thank you, sir," said Bassett. He gave a slow glance at the window, and, arranging the cheques neatly, turned toward the door.

"Will Mr. Hartley be long?" inquired Joan, turning round.

"Mr. Hartley, miss?" said Bassett, pausing, with his hand on the knob. "Mr. Hartley left half an hour ago."

Mr. Vyner, who felt the eyes of Miss Hartley fixed upon him, resisted by a supreme effort the impulse to look at her in return.

"Bassett!" he said, sharply.

"Sir?" said the other.. "Didn't you," said Mr. Vyner, with a fine and growing note of indignation in his voice—"didn't you tell Mr. Hartley that Miss Hartley was here waiting for him?"

"No, sir," said Bassett, gazing at certain mysterious workings of the junior partner's face with undisguised amazement. "I—"

"Do you mean to tell me," demanded Mr. Vyner, looking at him with great significance, "that you forgot?"

"No, sir," said Bassett; "I didn't—"

"That will do," broke in Mr. Vyner, imperiously. "That will do. You can go."

"But," said the amazed youth, "how could I tell—"

"That—will—do," said Mr. Vyner, very distinctly.

"I don't want any excuses. You can go at once. And the next time you are told to deliver a message, please don't forget. Now go."

With a fine show of indignation he thrust the gasping Bassett from the room.

He rose from his chair and, with a fine show of indignation, thrust the gasping Bassett from the room, and then turned to face the girl.

"I am so sorry," he began. "That stupid boy—you see how stupid he is—"

"It doesn't matter, thank you," said Joan. "It—it wasn't very important."

"He doesn't usually forget things," murmured Mr. Vyner. "I wish now," he added, truthfully, "that I had told Mr. Hartley myself."

He held the door open for her, and, still expressing his regret, accompanied her down-stairs to the door. Miss Hartley, somewhat embarrassed, and a prey to suspicions which maidenly modesty forbade her to voice, listened in silence.

"Next time you come," said Mr. Vyner, pausing just outside the door, "I hope—"

Something dropped between them, and fell with a little tinkling crash on to the pavement. Mr. Vyner stooped, and, picking up a pair of clumsily fashioned spectacles, looked swiftly up at the office window.

"Bassett," he said, involuntarily.

He stood looking at the girl, and trying in vain to think of something to say. Miss Hartley, with somewhat more colour than usual, gave him a little bow and hurried off.

CHAPTER V

Smiling despite herself as she thought over the events of the afternoon, Joan Hartley walked thoughtfully homeward. Indignation at Mr. Vyner's presumption was mingled with regret that a young man of undeniably good looks and somewhat engaging manners should stoop to deceit. The fact that people are considered innocent until proved guilty did not concern her. With scarcely any hesitation she summed up against him, the only thing that troubled her being what sentence to inflict, and how to inflict it. She wondered what excuse he could make for such behaviour, and then blushed hotly as she thought of the one he would probably advance. Confused at her own thoughts, she quickened her pace, in happy ignorance of the fact that fifty yards behind her Captain Trimblett and her father, who had witnessed with great surprise her leave-taking of Mr. Vyner, were regulating their pace by hers.

"She's a fine girl," said the captain, after a silence that had endured long enough to be almost embarrassing. "A fine girl, but—"

He broke off, and completed his sentence by a shake of the head.

"She must have come for me," said Hartley, "and he happened to be standing there and told her I had gone."

"No doubt," said the captain, dryly. "That's why she went scurrying off as though she had got a train to catch, and he stood there all that time looking after her. And, besides, every time he sees me, in some odd fashion your name crops up."

"My name?" said the other, in surprise.

"Your name," repeated the captain, firmly, "Same as Joan's, ain't it? The after-part of it, anyway. That's the attraction. Talk all round you—and I talk all round you, too. Nobody'd dream you'd got a daughter to hear the two of us talk—sometimes. Other times, if I bring her name in, they'd think you'd got nothing else."

Mr. Hartley glanced at him uneasily. "Perhaps—" he began.

"There's no 'perhaps' about it," said the masterful captain. "If you're not very careful there'll be trouble. You know what Mr. John is—he's got big ideas, and the youngster is as obstinate as a mule."

"It's all very well," said Hartley, "but how can I be careful? What can I do? Besides, I dare say you are making mountains of mole-heaps; she probably hurried off thinking to catch me up."

Captain Trimblett gave a little dry cough. "Ask her," he said, impressively.

"I'm not going to put any such ideas into her head," said his friend.

"Sound her, then," said the captain. "This is the way I look at it. We all think he is a very nice fellow, don't we?"

"He is," said Hartley, decidedly.

"And we all think she's a splendid girl, don't we?" continued the other.

"Something of the sort," said Hartley, smiling.

"There you are, then," said the captain, triumphantly. "What is more likely than that they should think the same of each other? Besides, I know what he thinks; I can read him like a book."

"You can't read Joan, though," said the other. "Why, she often puzzles me."

"I can try," said the captain. "I haven't known her all these years for nothing. Now, don't tell her we saw her. You leave her to me—and listen."

"Better leave her alone," said Hartley.

The captain, who was deep in thought, waved the suggestion aside. He walked the remainder of the way in silence, and even after they were in the house was so absorbed in his self-appointed task, and so vague in his replies, that Joan, after offering him the proverbial penny for his thoughts, suggested to her father in a loud whisper that he had got something in mind.

"Thinking of the ships he has lost," she said, in a still louder whisper.

The captain smiled and shook his head at her.

"Couldn't lose a ship if I tried," he said, nudging Hartley to call his attention to what was to follow. "I was saying so to Mr. Robert only yesterday!"

His voice was so deliberate, and his manner so significant, that Miss Hartley looked up in surprise. Then she coloured furiously as she saw both gentlemen eying her with the air of physicians on the lookout for unfavourable symptoms. Anger only deepened her colour, and an unladylike and unfilial yearning to bang their two foolish heads together possessed her. Explanations were impossible, and despite her annoyance she almost smiled as she saw the concern in the eye the captain turned on her father.

"Saying so only yesterday," repeated the former, "to Mr. Robert."

"I saw him this afternoon," said Joan, with forced composure. "I went up to father's room and found him there. Why didn't you tell me you had given up your room, father?"

Mr. Hartley pleaded in excuse that he thought he had told her, and was surprised at the vehemence of her denial. With a slightly offended air he pointed out that it was a very small matter after all.

"There is nothing to be annoyed about," he said.

"You went there to see me, and, not finding me there, came down again."

"Ye-es," said Joan, thoughtfully.

"Just put her head in at the door and fled," explained the captain, still watching her closely.

Miss Hartley appeared not to have heard him.

"Came down three stairs at a time," he continued, with a poor attempt at a chuckle.

"I was there about half an hour waiting for father," said Joan, eying him very steadily. "I thought that he was in the other office. Is there anything else I can tell you?"

The captain collapsed suddenly, and, turning a red face upon Hartley, appealed to him mutely for succour.

"Me?" he spluttered, feebly. "I—I don't want to know anything. Your father thought—"

"I didn't think anything," said Hartley, with some haste.

The captain eyed him reproachfully. "I thought your father thought—" he began, and, drawing out a large handkerchief, blew his nose violently.

"Yes?" said Joan, still very erect.

"That is all," said the captain, with an air of dignity.

He brushed some imaginary atoms from his beard, and, finding the girl's gaze still somewhat embarrassing, sought to relieve the tension.

"I've known you since you were five," he said, with inconsequent pathos.

"I know," said Joan, smiling, and putting her hand on his broad shoulder. "You're a dear old stupid; that is all."

"Always was," said the relieved captain, "from a child."

He began, with a cheerful countenance, to narrate anecdotes of his stupidity until, being interrupted by Hartley with one or two choice examples that he had forgotten, he rose and muttered something about seeing the garden. His progress was stayed by a knock at the front door and an intimation from Rosa that he was wanted.

"My bo'sun," he said, reentering the room with a letter. "Excuse me."

He broke the seal, and turned to Hartley with a short laugh. "Peter Truefitt," he said, "wants me to meet him at nine o'clock and go home together, pretending that he has been here with me. Peter is improving."

"But he can't go on like this forever," said his scandalized friend.

"He's all right," said the captain, with a satisfied wink. "I'm looking after him. I'm stage-manager. I'll see—"

His voice faltered, and then died away as he caught Miss Hartley's eye and noticed the air of artless astonishment with which she was regarding him.

"Always was from a child," she quoted.

The captain ignored her.

"I'll just give Walters a note," he said, turning to Hartley with some dignity. "You don't mind his waiting?"

He turned to a small writing-table, and with an air of preoccupation, assumed for Miss Hartley's benefit, began to try a pen on his thumb-nail. Hartley, going to the door, sent the boatswain off to the kitchen for a glass of ale.

"Or perhaps you prefer tea?" he added, thoughtfully.

"Ale will do, sir," said Mr. Walters, humbly.

He walked to the kitchen, and, pushing the door open softly, went in. Rosa Jelks, who was sitting down reading, put aside her book and smiled welcome.

"Sit down," she said, patronizingly; "sit down."

"I was going to," said Mr. Walters. "I'm to 'ave a glass of ale."

"Say 'please,'" said Rosa, shaking her yellow locks at him, and rising to take a glass from the dresser.

She walked into the scullery humming a tune, and the pleasant sound of beer falling into a glass fell on the boatswain's ears. He stroked his small black moustache and smiled.

"Would you like me to take a sip at the glass first?" inquired Rosa, coming back carefully with a brimming glass, "just to give it a flavour?"

Mr. Walters stared at her in honest amazement. After a moment he remarked gruffly that the flavour of the ale itself was good enough for him. Rosa's eyes sparkled.

"Just a sip," she pleaded.

"Go on, then," said Mr. Walters, grudgingly.

"Chin, chin!" said Rosa.

The boatswain's face relaxed. Then it hardened suddenly and a dazed look crept into his eyes as Rosa, drinking about two-thirds of the ale, handed him the remainder.

"That's for your impudence," she said, sharply. "I don't like beer."

Mr. Walters, still dazed, finished the beer without a word and placed the glass on the table. A faint sigh escaped him, but that was all.

"Bear!" said Rosa, making a face at him.

She looked at his strong, lean face and powerful figure approvingly, but the bereaved boatswain took no notice.

"Bear!" said Rosa again.

She patted her hair into place, and, in adjusting a hair-pin, permitted a long, thick tress to escape to her shoulder. She uttered a little squeal of dismay.

"False, ain't it?" inquired Mr. Walters, regarding her antics with some amazement.

"False!" exclaimed Rosa. "Certainly not. Here! Tug!"

She presented her shoulder to the boatswain, and he, nothing loath, gave a tug, animated by the loss of two-thirds of a glass of beer. The next instant a loud slap rang through the kitchen.

"And I'd do it again for two pins," said the outraged damsel, as she regarded him with watering eyes. "Brute!"

She turned away, and, pink with annoyance, proceeded to arrange her hair in a small cracked glass that hung by the mantel-piece.

"I 'ad a cousin once," said Mr. Walters, thoughtfully, "that used to let her 'air down and sit on it. Tall gal, too, she was."

"So can I," snapped Rosa, rolling the tress up on her finger, holding it in place, and transfixing it with a hair-pin.

"H'm," said the boatswain.

"What d'ye mean by that?" demanded Rosa, sharply. "Do you mean to say I can't?"

"You might if you cut it off first," conceded Mr. Walters.

"Cut it off?" said Rosa, scornfully. "Here! Look here!"

She dragged out her hair-pins and with a toss of her head sent the coarse yellow locks flying. Then, straightening them slightly, she pulled out a chair and confronted him triumphantly. And at that moment the front-room bell rang.

"That's for you," said Mr. Walters, pointedly.

Rosa, who was already back at the glass, working with feverish haste, made no reply. The bell rang again, and a third time, Rosa finally answering it in a coiffure that looked like a hastily constructed bird's nest.

"There's your letter," she said, returning with a face still flushed. "Take it and go."

"Thankee," said the boatswain. "Was they very frightened?"

"Take it and go," repeated Rosa, with cold dignity. "Your young woman might be expecting you; pity to keep her waiting."

"I ain't got a young woman," said Mr. Walters, slowly.

"You surprise me!" said Rosa, with false astonishment.

"I never would 'ave one," said the boatswain, rising, and placing the letter in his breast-pocket. "I've got along all right for thirty years without 'em, and I ain't going to begin now."

"You must have broke a lot of hearts with disappointment," said Rosa.

"I never could see anything in young wimmen," said the boatswain, musingly. "Silly things, most of 'em. Always thinking about their looks; especially them as haven't got none."

He took up the empty glass and toyed with it thoughtfully.

"It's no good waiting," said Rosa; "you won't get no more beer; not if you stay here all night."

"So long!" said the boatswain, still playing with the glass. "So long! I know one or two that'll 'ave a fit pretty near when I tell 'em about you sitting on your 'air."

He put up his left arm instinctively, but Miss Jelks by a supreme effort maintained her calmness. Her eyes and colour were beyond her control, but her voice remained steady.

"So long!" she said, quietly. She took the glass from him and smiled. "If you like to wait a moment, I'll get you a little drop more," she said, graciously.

"Here's luck!" said Mr. Walters, as she returned with the glass. He drank it slowly and then, wiping his lips with the back of his hand, stood regarding her critically.

"Well, so long!" he said again, and, before the astonished maiden could resist, placed a huge arm about her neck and kissed her.

"You do that again, if you dare!" she gasped, indignantly, as she broke loose and confronted him. "The idea!"

"I don't want to do it agin," said the boatswain. "I've 'ad a glass of ale, and you've 'ad a kiss. Now we're quits."

He wiped his mouth on the back of his hand again and walked off with the air of a man who has just discharged an obligation. He went out the back way, and Rosa, to whom this sort of man was an absolutely new experience, stood gazing after him dumbly. Recovering herself, she followed him to the gate, and, with a countenance on which amazement still lingered, stood watching his tall figure up the road.

CHAPTER VI

"Work!" said Mr. Robert Vyner, severely, as he reclined in a deck-chair on the poop of the Indian Chief and surveyed his surroundings through half-closed eyes. "Work! It's no good sitting here idling while the world's work awaits my attention."

Captain Trimblett, who was in a similar posture a yard away, assented. He also added that there was "nothing like it."

"There's no play without work," continued Mr. Vyner, in a spirit of self-admonition.

The captain assented again. "You said something about work half an hour ago," he remarked.

"And I meant it," said Mr. Vyner; "only in unconscious imitation I dozed off. What I really want is for somebody to take my legs, somebody else my shoulders, and waft me gently ashore."

"I had a cook o' mine put ashore like that once," said Captain Trimblett, in a reminiscent voice; "only I don't know that I would have called it 'wafting,' and, so far as my memory goes, he didn't either. He had a lot to say about it, too."

Mr. Vyner, with a noisy yawn, struggled out of his chair and stood adjusting his collar and waistcoat.

"If I couldn't be a chrysalis," he said, slowly, as he looked down at the recumbent figure of the captain, "do you know what I would like to be?"

"I've had a very hard day's work," said the other, defensively, as he struggled into a sitting posture— "very hard. And I was awake half the night with the toothache."

"That isn't an answer to my question," said Mr. Vyner, gently. "But never mind; try and get a little sleep now; try and check that feverish desire for work, which is slowly, very, very slowly, wearing you to skin and bone. Think how grieved the firm would be if the toothache carried you off one night. Why not go below and turn in now? It's nearly five o'clock."

"Couldn't sleep if I did," replied the captain, gravely. "Besides, I've got somebody coming aboard to have tea with me this afternoon."

"All right, I'm going," said Robert, reassuringly. "Nobody I know, I suppose?"

"No," said the captain. "Not exactly," he added, with a desire of being strictly accurate.

Mr. Vyner became thoughtful. The captain's reticence, coupled with the fact that he had made two or three attempts to get rid of him that afternoon, was suspicious. He wondered whether Joan Hartley was the expected guest; the captain's unwillingness to talk whenever her name came up having by no means escaped him. And once or twice the captain had, with unmistakable meaning, dropped hints as to the progress made by Mr. Saunders in horticulture and other pursuits. At the idea of this elderly mariner indulging in matrimonial schemes with which he had no sympathy, he became possessed with a spirit of vindictive emulation.

"It seems like a riddle; you've excited my curiosity," he said, as he threw himself back in the chair again and looked at the gulls wheeling lazily overhead. "Let me see whether I can guess—I'll go as soon as I have."

"'Tisn't worth guessing," said Captain Trimblett, with a touch of brusqueness.

"Don't make it too easy," pleaded Mr. Vyner. "Guess number one: a lady?"

The captain grunted.

"A widow," continued Mr. Vyner, in the slow, rapt tones of a clairvoyant. "The widow!"

"What do you mean by the widow?" demanded the aroused captain.

"The one you are always talking about," replied Mr. Vyner, winking at the sky.

"Me!" said the captain, purpling. "I don't talk about her. You don't hear me talk about her. I'm not always talking about anybody. I might just have mentioned her name when talking about Truefitt's troubles; that's all."

"That's what I meant," said Robert Vyner, with an air of mild surprise.

"Well, it's not her," said the captain, shortly.

"Somebody I know, but not exactly," mused Robert. "Somebody I know, but—Let me think."

He closed his eyes in an effort of memory, and kept them shut so long that the captain, anxious to get him away before his visitor's arrival, indulged in a loud and painful fit of coughing. Mr. Vyner's eyes remained closed.

"Any more guesses?" inquired the captain, loudly.

Mr. Vyner, slept on. Gulls mewed overhead; a rattle of cranes sounded from the quays, and a conversation—mostly in hoarse roars—took place between the boatswain in the bows and an elderly man ashore, but he remained undisturbed. Then he sprang up so suddenly that he nearly knocked his chair over, and the captain, turning his head after him in amaze, saw Joan Hartley standing at the edge of the quay.

Before he could interfere Mr. Vyner, holding her hand with anxious solicitude, was helping her aboard. Poised for a moment on the side of the ship, she sprang lightly to the deck, and the young man, relinquishing her hand with some reluctance, followed her slowly toward the captain.

Ten minutes later, by far the calmest of the three, he sat at tea in the small but comfortable saloon. How he got there Captain Trimblett could not exactly remember. Mr. Vyner had murmured something about a slight headache, due in his opinion to the want of a cup of tea, and, even while talking about going home to get it, had in an abstracted fashion drifted down the companion-way.

"I feel better already," he remarked, as he passed his cup up to Miss Hartley to be refilled. "It's wonderful what a cup of tea will do."

"It has its uses," said the captain, darkly.

He took another cup himself and sat silent and watchful, listening to the conversation of his guests. A slight appearance of reserve on Miss Hartley's part, assumed to remind Mr. Vyner of his bad behaviour on the occasion of their last meeting, was dispelled almost immediately. Modesty, tinged with respectful admiration, was in every glance and every note of his voice. When she discovered that a man who had asked for his tea without sugar had drunk without remark a cup containing three lumps, she became thoughtful.

"Why didn't you tell me?" she asked, in concern.

Modesty and Mr. Vyner—never boon companions—parted company.

"I thought you had given me the wrong cup," he said, simply.

The explanation seemed to Captain Trimblett quite inadequate. He sat turning it over in his mind, and even the rising colour in Miss Hartley's cheek did not serve to enlighten him. But he was glad to notice that she was becoming reserved again. Mr. Vyner noticed it, too, and, raging inwardly against a tongue which was always striving after his undoing, began with a chastened air to criticise the architecture of the new chapel in Porter Street. Architecture being a subject of which the captain knew nothing, he discussed it at great length, somewhat pleased to find that both his listeners were giving him their undivided attention.

He was glad to notice, when they went up on deck again, that his guests had but little to say to each other, and, with a view to keeping them apart as much as possible, made no attempt to detain her when Joan rose and said that she must be going. She shook hands and then turned to Mr. Vyner.

"Oh, I must be going, too," said that gentleman.

He helped her ashore and, with a wave of his hand to Captain Trimblett, set off by her side. At the bridge, where their ways homeward diverged, Joan half stopped, but Mr. Vyner, gazing straight ahead, kept on.

"Fine chap, Captain Trimblett," he said, suddenly.

"He is the kindest man I know," said Joan, warmly.

Mr. Vyner sang his praises for three hundred yards, secretly conscious that his companion was thinking of ways and means of getting rid of him. The window of a confectioner's shop at last furnished the necessary excuse.

"I have got a little shopping to do," she said, diving in suddenly. "Good-by."

"The 'good-by' was so faint that it was apparent to her as she stood in the shop and gave a modest order for chocolates that he had not heard it. She bit her lip, and after a glance at the figure outside, added to her order a large one for buns. She came out of the shop with a bag overflowing with them.

"Let me," said Mr. Vyner, hastily.

Miss Hartley handed them over at once, and, walking by his side, strove hard to repress malicious smiles. She walked slowly and gave appraising glances at shop windows, pausing finally at a greengrocer's to purchase some bananas. Mr. Vyner, with the buns held in the hollow of his arm, watched her anxiously, and his face fell as she agreed with the greengrocer as to the pity of spoiling a noble bunch he was displaying. Insufficiently draped in a brown-paper bag, it took Mr. Vyner's other arm.

"You are quite useful," said Miss Hartley, with a bright smile.

Mr. Vyner returned the smile, and in bowing to an acquaintance nearly lost a bun. He saved it by sheer sleight of hand, and noting that his companion was still intent on the shops, wondered darkly what further burdens were in store for him. He tried to quicken the pace, but Miss Hartley was not to be hurried.

"I must go in here, I think," she said, stopping in front of a draper's. "I sha'n't be long."

Mr. Vyner took his stand by the window with his back to the passers-by, and waited. At the expiration of ten minutes he peeped in at the door, and saw Miss Hartley at the extreme end of the shop thoughtfully fingering bales of cloth. He sighed, and, catching sight of a small boy regarding him, had a sudden inspiration.

"Here! Would you like some buns, old chap?" he cried.

The child's eyes glistened.

"Take 'em," said Mr. Vyner, thankfully. "Don't drop 'em."

He handed them over and stood smiling benevolently as the small boy, with both arms clasped round the bag, went off hugging it to his bosom. Another urchin, who had been regarding the transaction with speechless envy, caught his eye. He beckoned him to him and, with a few kind words and a fatherly admonition not to make himself ill, presented him with the bananas. Then he drew a deep breath, and with a few kind words he presented him with the bananas assuming an expression of gravity befitting the occasion, braced himself for the inevitable encounter.

Five minutes later Miss Hartley, bearing a large and badly-tied parcel, came smiling out to him. The smile faded suddenly, and she stood regarding him in consternation.

"Why!" she began. "Where?"

Mr. Vyner eyed her carefully. "I gave 'em away," he said, slowly. "Two poor, hungry little chaps stood looking at me. I am awfully fond of children, and before I knew what I was doing—"

"I've no doubt," said Joan, bitterly, as she realized her defeat. "I've no doubt."

Mr. Vyner leaned toward the parcel. "Allow me," he murmured, politely.

"Thank you, Til carry it myself," said Joan, sharply.

Her taste for shopping had evaporated, and clutching her parcel she walked rapidly homeward. An occasional glance at her companion did not quite satisfy her that he was keeping his sense of humour under proper control. There was a twitching of his lips which might, she felt, in a little time become contagious. She averted her head.

"That's all right," said Mr. Vyner, with a sigh of relief. "I was half afraid that I had offended you."

CHAPTER VII

To the great relief of Mr. Truefitt's imagination, his sister suddenly ceased from all comment upon the irregularity of his hours. Unprepared, by the suddenness of the change, he recited mechanically, for the first day or two, the reasons he had invented for his lateness, but their reception was of so chilling a nature that his voice was scarcely audible at the finish. Indeed, when he came home one evening with a perfectly true story of a seaman stabbed down by the harbour, Mrs. Chinnery yawned three times during the narration, and Captain Trimblett shook his head at him.

"True or not," said the latter, after Mrs. Chinnery had left the room, "it doesn't matter. It isn't worth while explaining when explanations are not asked for."

"Do you think she knows?" inquired Mr. Truefitt, with bated voice.

"She knows something," replied the captain. "I believe she knows all about it, else she wouldn't keep so quiet. Why not tell her straight out? Tell her when she comes in, and get it over. She's got to know some day."

"Poor Susan!" said Mr. Truefitt, with feeling. "I'm afraid she'll feel it. It's not nice to have to leave home to make room for somebody else. And she won't stay in it with another woman, I'm certain."

"Here she comes," said the captain, getting up. "I'll go out for a little stroll, and when I come back I shall expect to find you've made a clean breast of it."

Mr. Truefitt put out a hand as though to detain him, and then, thinking better of it, nodded at him with an air of great resolution, and puffed furiously at his pipe. Under cover of clouds of smoke he prepared for the encounter.

Closing the door gently behind him, the captain, after a moment's indecision, drifted down the road. A shower of rain had brought out sweet odours from the hedgerow opposite, and a touch of salt freshened the breeze that blew up the river. Most of the inhabitants of the Vale were in bed, and the wet road was lonely under the stars. He walked as far as a little bridge spanning a brook that ran into the river, and seating himself on the low parapet smoked thoughtfully. His mind went back to his own marriage many years before, and to his children, whom he had placed, on his wife's death, with a second cousin in London. An unusual feeling of loneliness possessed him. He smoked a second pipe and then, knocking the ashes out on the bridge, walked slowly homeward.

Mr. Truefitt, who was sitting alone, looked up as he entered and smiled vaguely.

"All right?" queried the captain, closing the door and crossing to a chair.

"Right as ninepence," said Mr. Truefitt. "I've been worrying myself all this time for nothing. Judging by her manner, she seemed to think it was the most natural and proper thing in the world."

"So it is," said the captain, warmly.

"She talked about it as calmly as though she had a brother married every week," continued Mr. Truefitt. "I don't suppose she has quite realized it yet."

"I don't know that I have," said the captain. "This has been the only home I've had for the last ten years; and I feel leaving it, what must it be for her?"

Mr. Truefitt shook his head.

"I'm beginning to feel old," said the captain, "old and lonely. Changes like this bring it home to one."

He took out his pouch, and shaking his head solemnly began to fill his pipe again.

"You ought to follow my example," said Mr. Truefitt, eagerly.

"Too old," said the captain.

"Nonsense!" said the other. "And the older you get, the lonelier you'll feel. Mind that!"

"I shall go and live with my boys and girls when I leave the sea," said the captain.

"They'll probably be married themselves by that time," said his comforter.

He rose, and, going to an old corner cupboard, took out a bottle of whiskey and a couple of glasses and put them on the table. The captain, helping himself liberally, emptied his glass to Miss Willett.

"She's coming to tea on Friday, with her mother," said Mr. Truefitt.

Captain Trimblett took some more whiskey and solemnly toasted Mrs. Willett. He put his glass down, and lighting his pipe, which had gone out, beamed over at his friend.

"Are there any more in the family?" he inquired.

"There's an uncle," said Mr. Truefitt, slowly, "and—"

"One at a time," said the captain, stopping him with one hand raised, while he helped himself to some more whiskey with the other. "The uncle!"

He drank the third glass slowly, and, sinking back in his chair, turned to his friend with a countenance somewhat flushed and wreathed in smiles.

"Who else?" he inquired.

"No more to-night," said Mr. Truefitt, firmly, as he got up and put the bottle back in the cupboard. He came back slowly, and, resuming his seat, gazed in a meditative fashion at his friend.

"Talking about your loneliness—" he began.

"My loneliness?" repeated the captain, staring at "You were talking about feeling lonely," Mr. Truett reminded him.

He proceeded with almost equal care to assist her mother

"So I was," said the captain. "So I was. You're quite right; but it's all gone now. It's wonderful what a little whiskey will do."

"Wonderful what a lot will do," said Mr. Truefitt, with sudden asperity. "You were talking about your loneliness, and I was advising you to get married."

"So you were," said the captain, nodding at him. "Good-night."

He went off to bed with a suddenness that was almost disconcerting. Thus deserted, Mr. Truefitt finished his whiskey and water and, his head full of plans for the betterment of everybody connected with him, blew out the lamp and went upstairs.

Owing possibly to his efforts in this direction Captain Trimblett and Mrs. Chinnery scarcely saw him until Friday afternoon, when he drove up in a fly, and, after handing out Miss Willett with great tenderness, proceeded with almost equal care to assist her mother. The latter, a fragile little old lady, was at once conducted to a chair and, having been comfortably seated was introduced to Mrs. Chinnery.

"It's a long way," she said, as her daughter divested her of her bonnet and shawl, "but Cissie would insist on my coming, and I suppose, after all, it's only right I should."

"Of course, mother," said Miss Willett, hurriedly.

"Right is right," continued the old lady, "after all is said and done. And I'm sure Mr. Truefitt has been to ours often enough."

Mr. Truefitt coughed, and the captain—a loyal friend—assisted him.

"Night after night," said the old lady, during a brief interval.

Mr. Truefitt, still coughing slightly, began to place chairs at a table on which, as the captain presently-proved to his own dissatisfaction, there was not even; room for a pair of elbows. At the last moment the seating arrangements had to be altered owing to a leg of the table which got in the way of Mrs. Willett's. The captain, in his anxiety to be of service, lowered a leaf of the table too far, and an avalanche of food descended to the floor.

"It don't matter," said Mrs. Chinnery, in a voice that belied her words. "Captain Trimblett is always doing something like that. The last time we had visitors he—"

"Kept on eating the cake after she had shaken her head at me," interrupted the captain, who was busy picking up the provisions.

"Nothing of the kind," cried Mrs. Chinnery, who was in no mood for frivolity. "I shouldn't think of doing such a thing," she added, turning to Mrs. Willett, as the lady allowed herself to be placed in a more convenient position. "It's all Captain Trimblett's nonsense."

Mrs. Willett listened politely, "It is annoying, though," she remarked.

"He might eat all the cake in the house for what I care," said Mrs. Chinnery, turning very red, and raising her voice a little.

"As a matter of fact I don't like cake," said the captain, who was becoming uncomfortable.

"Perhaps it was something else," said the excellent Mrs. Willett, with the air of one assisting to unravel a mystery.

Mrs. Chinnery, who was pouring out tea, glared at her in silence. She also spared a glance for Captain Trimblett, which made that gentleman seriously uneasy. With an idea of turning the conversation into safer and more agreeable channels, he called the old lady's attention to a pencil drawing of a ruined castle which adorned the opposite wall. Mrs. Willett's first remark was that it had no roof.

"It's a ruin," said the captain; "done by Mrs. Chinnery."

The faded blue eyes behind the gold-rimmed spectacles inspected it carefully. "Done when she was a child—of course?" said Mrs. Willett.

"Eighteen," said Mrs. Chinnery, in a deep voice.

"I'm no judge of such things," said the old lady, shaking her head. "I only know what I like; but I dare say it's very clever."

She turned to help herself from a plate that the captain was offering her, and, finding that it contained cake, said that she would prefer bread and butter.

"Not that I don't like cake," she said. "As a rule I am rather partial to it."

"Well, have some now," said the unfortunate captain, trying to avoid Mrs. Chinnery's eye.

"Bread and butter, please," said Mrs. Willett, with quiet decision.

The captain passed it, and after a hopeless glance at Mr. Truefitt and Miss Willett, who were deep in the enjoyment of each other's society, returned to the subject of art.

"If I could draw like that, ma'am," he said, with a jerk of his head toward the ruined castle, "I should give up the sea."

Mrs. Willett inspected it again, even going to the length of taking off her glasses and polishing them, with a view to doing perfect justice to the subject. "Would you really?" she said, when she had finished.

The captain made no reply. He sat appalled at the way in which the old lady was using him to pay off some of the debt that she fancied was due to Mrs. Chinnery.

"You must see some of my daughter's pictures," she said, turning to him. "Fruit and birds mostly, in oil colours. But then, of course, she had good masters. There's one picture—let me see!"

She sat considering, and began to reel off the items on her fingers as she enumerated them. "There's a plate of oranges, with a knife and fork, a glass, a bottle, two and a half walnuts and bits of shell, three-quarters of an apple, a pipe, a cigar, a bunch of grapes, and a green parrot looking at it all with his head on one side."

"And very natural of him, too," murmured Mrs. Chinnery.

"It's coming here," interposed Mr. Truefitt, suddenly. "It belongs to Mrs. Willett, but she has given it to us. I wonder which will be the best place for it?"

The old lady looked round the room. "It will have to hang there," she said, pointing to the "Eruption of Vesuvius," "where that beehive is."

"Bee—!" exclaimed the startled captain. He bent toward her and explained.

"Oh, well, it don't matter," said the old lady. "I thought it was a beehive—it looks like one; and I can't see what's written under it from here. But that's where Cecilia's picture must go."

She made one or two other suggestions with regard to the rearrangement of the pictures, and then, having put her hand to the plough, proceeded to refurnish the room. And for her own private purposes she affected to think that Mr. Truefitt's taste was responsible for the window-curtains.

"Mother has got wonderful taste," said Miss Willett, looking round. "All over Salthaven her taste has become a—a—"

"Byword," suggested Mrs. Chinnery.

"Proverb," said Miss Willett. "Are you feeling too warm, mother?" she asked, eying the old lady with sudden concern.

"A little," said Mrs. Willett. "I suppose it's being used to big rooms. I always was one for plenty of space. It doesn't matter—don't trouble."

"It's no trouble," said Captain Trimblett, who was struggling with the window. "How is that?" he inquired, opening it a little at the top and returning to his seat.

"There is a draught down the back of my neck," said Mrs. Willett; "but don't trouble about me if the others like it. If I get a stiff neck Cecilia can rub it for me when I get home with a little oil of camphor."

"Yes, mother," said Miss Willett.

"I once had a stiff neck for three weeks," said Mrs. Willett.

The captain rose again and, with a compassionate glance at Mr. Truefitt, closed the window.

"One can't have everything in this world," said the old lady; "it ought to be a very cosey room in winter, You can't get too far away from the fire, I mean."

"It has done for us for a good many years now," said Mrs. Chinnery. "I've never heard Peter complain."

"He'd never complain," said Mrs. Willett, with a fond smile at her prospective son-in-law. "Why, he wouldn't know he was uncomfortable unless somebody told him."

Mrs. Chinnery pushed back her chair with a grating noise, strangely in harmony with her feelings, and, after a moment's pause to control her voice, suggested that the gentlemen should take the visitors round the garden while she cleared away—a proposal accepted by all but Mrs. Willett.

"I'll stay here and watch you," she said.

Captain Trimblett accompanied Mr. Truefitt and Miss Willett into the garden, and after pointing out the missing beauties of a figure-head in the next garden but one, and calling attention to the geraniums next door, left the couple to themselves. Side by side in the little arbour they sat gazing on to the river and conversing in low tones of their future happiness.

For some time the captain idled about the garden, keeping as far away from the arbour as possible, and doing his best to suppress a decayed but lively mariner named Captain Sellers, who lived two doors off. Among other infirmities the latter was nearly stone-deaf, and, after giving up as hopeless the attempt to make him understand that Mr. Truefitt and Miss Willett were not, the captain at last sought shelter in the house.

He found the table clear and a bowl of flowers placed in the exact centre. On opposite sides of the room, each with her hands folded in her lap, and both sitting bolt upright, Mrs. Willett and Mrs. Chinnery confronted each other. With a muttered reference to his ship, the captain took up his stick and fled.

He spent the evening in the billiard-room of the Golden Fleece, and did not return until late. A light in the room up-stairs and a shadow on the blind informed him that Mrs. Chinnery had retired. He stepped in quietly, and closed the door behind him. Mr. Truefitt, a picture of woe, was sitting in his usual place at the corner of the stove, and a supper-table, loaded with food, was untouched.

"Gone?" inquired the captain, scenting disaster.

"Some time ago," said Mr. Truefitt. "They wouldn't stay to supper. I wish you had been here to persuade them."

"I wish I had," said the captain, untruthfully.

He gave utterance to a faint sigh in token of sympathy with Mr. Truefitt's evident distress, and drew a chair to the table. He shook his head, and with marvellous accuracy, considering that his gaze was fastened on a piece of cold beef, helped himself to a wedge of steak-pie. He ate with an appetite, and after pouring out and drinking a glass of ale gazed again at the forlorn figure of Mr. Truefitt.

"Words?" he breathed, in a conspirator's whisper.

The other shook his head. "No; they were very polite," he replied, slowly.

The captain nearly emitted a groan. He checked it with two square inches of pie-crust.

"A misunderstanding," said Mr. Truefitt.

The captain said "Ah!" It was all he could say for the moment.

"A misunderstanding," said the other. "I misled Mrs. Willett," he added, in a tense whisper.

"Good heavens!" said the captain.

"She had always understood—from me," continued Mr. Truefitt, "that when I married Susanna would go. I always thought she would. Anybody who knew Susanna would have thought so. You would—wouldn't you?"

"In the ordinary way—yes," said the captain; "but circumstances alter cases."

"It came out—in conversation," said the hapless Mr. Truefitt, "that Susanna wouldn't dream of leaving me. It also came out that Mrs. Willett wouldn't dream of letting Cecilia marry me till she does. What's to be done?"

The captain took a slice of beef to assist thought. "You must have patience," he said, sagely.

"Patience!" said Mr. Truefitt, with unusual heat. "Patience be damned! I'm fifty-two! And Cecilia's thirty-nine!"

"Time flies!" said the captain, who could think of nothing else to say.

Mr. Truefitt looked at him almost savagely. Then he sank back in his chair.

"It's a pity Susanna doesn't get married again," he said, slowly. "So far as I can see, that's the only way out of it. Cecilia said so to me just as she was leaving."

"Did she?" said the captain. He looked thoughtful, and Mr. Truefitt watched him anxiously. For some time he seemed undecided, and then, with the resolute air of a man throwing appearances to the winds, he drew an uncut tongue toward him and cut off a large slice.

CHAPTER VIII

Nearly a week had elapsed since Robert Vyner's failure to give satisfaction as a light porter, and in all that time, despite his utmost efforts, he had failed to set eyes on Joan Hartley. In the hope of a chance encounter he divided his spare time between the narrow, crooked streets of Salthaven and the deck of the Indian Chief, but in vain. In a mysterious and highly unsatisfactory fashion Miss Hartley seemed to have vanished from the face of the earth.

In these circumstances he manifested a partiality for the company of Mr. Hartley that was a source of great embarrassment to that gentleman, whose work rapidly accumulated while he sat in his old office discussing a wide range of subjects, on all of which the junior partner seemed equally at home and inclined to air views of the most unorthodox description. He passed from topic to topic with bewildering facility, and one afternoon glided easily and naturally from death duties to insect powder, and from that to maggots in rose-buds, almost before his bewildered listener could take breath. From rose-buds he discoursed on gardening—a hobby to which he professed himself desirous of devoting such few hours as could be spared from his arduous work as a member of the firm.

"I hear that your garden is the talk of Salthaven," he remarked.

Mr. Hartley, justly surprised, protested warmly.

"That's what I heard," said Mr. Vyner, doggedly.

Mr. Hartley admitted that his borders were good. He also gave favourable mention to his roses.

"My favourite flower," said Mr. Vyner, with enthusiasm.

"I'll bring you a bunch to-morrow, if you will let me," said Mr. Hartley, rising and turning toward the door.

The other stopped him with outstretched hand. "No, don't do that," he said, earnestly. "I hate cutting flowers. It seems such a—a—desecration."

Mr. Hartley, quite unprepared for so much feeling on the subject, gazed at him in astonishment.

"I should like to see them, too," said Robert, musingly, "very much."

The chief clerk, with a little deprecatory cough, got close to the door as a dim idea that there might be something after all in Captain Trimblett's warnings occurred to him.

"Yours are mostly standard roses, aren't they?" said the persevering Robert.

"Mostly," was the reply.

Mr. Vyner regarded him thoughtfully. "I suppose you don't care to let people see them for fear they should learn your methods?" he said, at last.

Mr. Hartley, coming away from the door, almost stuttered in his haste to disclaim such ungenerous sentiments. "I am always glad to show them," he said, emphatically, "and to give any information I can."

"I should like to see them some time," murmured Robert.

The other threw caution to the winds. "Any time," he said, heartily.

Mr. Vyner thanked him warmly, and, having got what he wanted, placed no further obstacles in the way of his withdrawal. He bought a book entitled "Roses and How to Grow Them" the same afternoon and the next evening called to compare his knowledge with Mr. Hartley's.

Mr. Hartley was out; Miss Hartley was out; but at Rosa's invitation he went in to await their return. At her further suggestion—due to a habit she had of keeping her ears open and a conversation between her master and Captain Trimblett on the previous evening—he went into the garden to see the flowers.

"The other one's there," said Rosa, simply, as she showed him the way.

Mr. Vyner started, but a glance at Rosa satisfied him that there was all to lose and nothing to gain by demanding an explanation which she would be only too ready to furnish. With an air of cold dignity he strolled down the garden.

A young man squatting in a painful attitude at the edge of a flower-bed paused with his trowel in the air and eyed him with mingled consternation and disapproval. After allowing nearly a week to elapse since his last visit, Mr. Saunders, having mustered up sufficient courage to come round for another lesson in horticulture, had discovered to his dismay that both Mr. Hartley and his daughter had engagements elsewhere. That his evening should not be given over to disappointment entirely, however, the former had set him a long and arduous task before taking his departure.

"Don't let me interrupt you," said Mr. Vyner, politely, as the other rose and straightened himself. "What are you doing—besides decapitating worms?"

"Putting in these plants," said Mr. Saunders, resentfully.

Mr. Vyner eyed them with the eye of a connoisseur, and turning one over with his stick shook his head disparagingly. For some time he amused himself by walking up and down the garden inspecting the roses, and then, lighting a cigarette, threw himself at full length on to a garden bench that stood near Mr. Saunders and watched him at work.

"Fascinating pursuit," he remarked, affably.

Mr. Saunders grunted; Mr. Vyner blew out a thin thread of smoke toward the sky and pondered.

"Fine exercise; I wish I could get fond of it," he remarked.

"Perhaps you could if you tried," said the other, without looking round.

"After all," said Mr. Vyner, thoughtfully; "after all, perhaps it does one just as much good to watch other people at it. My back aches with watching you, and my knees are stiff with cramp. I suppose yours are, too?"

Mr. Saunders made no reply. He went on stolidly with his work until, reaching over too far with the trowel, he lost his balance and pitched forward on to his hands. Somewhat red in the face he righted himself, and knocking the mould off his hands, started once more.

"Try, try, try again," quoted the admiring onlooker.

"Perhaps you'd like to take a turn," said Mr. Saunders, looking round and speaking with forced politeness.

Mr. Vyner shook his head, and, helping himself to another cigarette, proffered the case to the worker, and, on that gentleman calling attention to the grimy condition of his hands, stuck one in his mouth and lit it for him. Considerably mollified by these attentions, the amateur gardener resumed his labours with a lighter heart.

Joan Hartley, returning half an hour later, watched them for some time from an upper window, and then, with a vague desire to compel the sprawling figure on the bench to get up and do a little work, came slowly down the garden.

"You are working too hard, Mr. Saunders," she remarked, after Mr. Vyner had shaken hands and the former had pleaded the condition of his.

"He likes it," said Mr. Vyner.

"At any rate, it has got to be finished," said Mr. Saunders.

Miss Hartley looked at them, and then at the work done and the heap of plants still to go in. She stood tapping the ground thoughtfully with her foot.

"I expect that we are only interrupting him by standing here talking to him," said Robert Vyner, considerately. "No doubt he is wishing us anywhere but here; only he is too polite to say so."

Ignoring Mr. Saunders's fervent protestations, he took a tentative step forward, as though inviting Miss Hartley to join him; but she stood firm.

"Will you give me the trowel, please?" she said, with sudden decision.

Before Mr. Saunders could offer any resistance she took it from him, and stooping gracefully prepared to dig. Mr. Vyner interposed with some haste.

"Allow me," he said.

Miss Hartley placed the trowel in his hands at once, and with her lips curved in a slight smile stood watching his efforts. By almost imperceptible degrees she drew away from him and, attended by the devoted Mr. Saunders, sauntered slowly about the garden. The worker, glaring sideways, watched them as they roamed from flower to flower. The low murmur of their voices floated on the still air, and once or twice he heard Miss Hartley laugh with great distinctness.

Apparently engrossed with his task, Mr. Vyner worked cheerfully for ten minutes. The hand that held the trowel was so far fairly clean, and he was about to use it to take out a cigarette when he paused, and a broad smile spread slowly over his features. He put down the trowel, and, burrowing in the wet earth with both hands, regarded the result with smiling satisfaction. The couple came toward him slowly, and Mr. Saunders smiled in his turn as he saw the state of the other's hands.

"I beg your pardon," said Mr. Vyner, standing up as Miss Hartley came close; "I wish you would do something for me."

"Yes?" said Joan.

"I want a cigarette."

The girl looked puzzled. "Yes?" she said again.

Mr. Vyner, grave as a judge, held up his disgraceful hands. "They are in a case in the inside pocket of my coat," he said, calmly.

Miss Hartley drew back a pace. "Perhaps Mr. Saunders could help you," she said, hastily.

Mr. Vyner shook his head. "His hands are worse than mine," he said, mournfully.

He held up his arm so that his coat opened a little more, and Miss Hartley, after a moment's hesitation, thrust a small hand into his pocket and drew out the case.

"To open it you press the catch," said Mr. Vyner.

Miss Hartley pressed, and the case flew open. She stood holding it before him, and Mr. Vyner, with a helpless gesture, again exhibited his hands.

"If you would complete your kindness by putting one in my mouth," he murmured.

For a few moments she stood in a state of dazed indecision; then, slowly extracting a cigarette from the case, she placed it between his lips with a little jab that made it a failure, as a smoke, from the first. Mr. Saunders, who had been watching events with a brooding eye, hastily struck a match and gave him a light, and Mr. Vyner, with an ill-concealed smile, bent down to his work again. He was pleased to notice that though the conversation between the others still proceeded, after a fitful fashion, Miss Hartley laughed no more.

He worked on steadily, and trampled ground and broken plants bore witness to his industry. He was just beginning to feel that he had done enough gardening for that day, when the return of Mr. Hartley brought welcome relief. The astonishment of the latter at finding this new and unlooked-for assistance was at first almost beyond words. When he could speak he thanked him brokenly for his trouble and, depriving him of his tools, took him indoors to wash.

"He means well," he said, slowly, after Mr. Vyner had at last taken his departure; "he means well, but I am afraid Mr. John wouldn't like it."

Miss Hartley flushed. "We didn't ask him to come," she said, with spirit.

"No," said her father, plucking at his beard, and regarding her with a troubled expression. "No; I'm afraid that he is one of those young men that don't want much asking."

CHAPTER IX

Owing possibly to the unaccustomed exercise, but probably to more sentimental reasons, Robert Vyner slept but poorly the night after his labours. He had explained his absence at the dinner-table by an airy reference to a long walk and a disquisition on the charms of the river by evening, an explanation which both Mr. Vyner and his wife had received with the silence it merited. It was evident that his absence had been the subject of some comment, but his father made no reference to it as they smoked a cigar together before retiring.

He awoke early in the morning and, after a vain attempt to get to sleep again, rose and dressed. Nobody else was stirring, and going quietly downstairs he took up a cap and went out.

Except for a labouring man or two tramping stolidly to work, the streets were deserted. The craft anchored in the river seemed asleep, and he stood for some time on the bridge idly watching the incoming tide. He lit his pipe and then, with a feeble endeavour to feel a little surprise at the fact, discovered that he was walking in the direction of Mr. Hartley's house.

His pace slackened as he neared it, and he went by gazing furtively at the drawn blinds of the front windows. A feeling of regret that Joan Hartley should be missing such a delightful morning would not be denied; in imagination he saw himself strolling by her side and pointing out to her the beauties of the most unfrequented portions of the river bank. A sudden superstitious trust in fate—caught possibly from Captain Trimblett—made him turn and walk slowly past the house again. With an idea of giving fate another chance he repeated the performance. In all he passed eight times, and was about to enter upon the ninth, when he happened to look across the road and saw, to his annoyance, the small figure of Bassett speeding toward him.

"He is not down yet, sir," said Bassett, respectfully.

Mr. Vyner suppressed his choler by an effort.

"Oh!" he said, stiffly. "Well?"

Bassett drew back in confusion. "I—I saw you walk up and down several times looking at the house, sir, and I thought it my duty to come and tell you," he replied.

Mr. Vyner regarded him steadfastly. "Thank you," he said, at last. "And how is it that you are out at such an early hour, prowling about like a raging lion looking for its breakfast?"

"I wasn't, sir," said Bassett; "I shall have my breakfast when I get home, at eight o'clock. I always get up at six; then I make sure of two hours in the fresh air."

"And what time do you close your eyes on the world and its vanities?" inquired Mr. Vyner, with an appearance of great interest.

"I always go to bed as the clock strikes ten, sir," said the youth.

"And suppose—suppose the clock should be wrong one day?" suggested the other, "would you apprehend any lasting injury to your constitution?"

"It couldn't be, sir," said Bassett; "I wind it myself."

Mr. Vyner regarded him more thoughtfully than before. "I can foresee," he said, slowly, "that you will grow up a great and good and wise man, unless—"

"Yes, sir," said Bassett, anxiously.

"Unless somebody kills you in the meantime," concluded Mr. Vyner. "It is not fair to tempt people beyond their strength, Bassett. Even a verdict of 'Justifiable homicide' might not quite ease the slayer's conscience."

"No, sir," said the perplexed youth.

Mr. Vyner suddenly dropped his bantering air.

"How was it I didn't see you?" he demanded, sternly.

"I don't think you looked my side of the road, sir," said Bassett. "You were watching Mr. Hartley's windows all the time; and, besides, I was behind that hedge."

He pointed to a well-trimmed privet hedge in a front garden opposite.

"Behind the hedge?" repeated the other, sharply. "What were you there for?"

"Watching a snail, sir," replied Bassett.

"A what?" inquired Mr. Vyner, raising his voice.

"A snail, sir," repeated the youth. "I've got a book on natural history, and I've just been reading about them. I saw this one as I was passing, and I went inside to study its habits. They are very interesting little things to watch—very."

Fortified by the approval of a conscience that never found fault, he met the searchlight gaze that the junior partner turned upon him without flinching. Quite calm, although somewhat puzzled by the other's manner, he stood awaiting his pleasure.

"Yes," said Robert Vyner, at last; "very interesting indeed, I should think; but you have forgotten one thing, Bassett. When secreted behind a hedge watching one of these diverting little—er—"

"Gasteropodous molluscs, sir," interjected Bassett, respectfully.

"Exactly," said the other. "Just the word I was trying to think of. When behind a hedge watching them it is always advisable to whistle as loudly and as clearly as you can."

"I never heard that, sir," said Bassett, more and more perplexed. "It's not in my book, but I remember once reading, when I was at school, that spiders are sometimes attracted by the sound of a flute."

"A flute would do," said Mr. Vyner, still watching him closely; "but a cornet would be better still. Good-morning."

He left Bassett gazing after him round-eyed, and, carefully refraining from looking at Hartley's windows, walked on at a smart pace. As he walked he began to wish that he had not talked so much; a vision of Bassett retailing the conversation of the morning to longer heads than his own in the office recurring to him with tiresome persistency. And, on the other hand, he regretted that he had not crossed the road and made sure that there was a snail.

Busy with his thoughts he tramped on mechanically, until, pausing on a piece of high ground to admire the view, he was surprised to see that the town lay so far behind. At the same time sudden urgent promptings from within bore eloquent testimony to the virtues of early rising and exercise as aids to appetite. With ready obedience he began to retrace his steps.

The business of the day was just beginning as he entered the outskirts of the town again. Blinds were drawn aside and maid-servants busy at front doors. By the time he drew near Laurel Lodge—the name was the choice of a former tenant—the work of the day had begun in real earnest. Instinctively slackening his pace, he went by the house with his eyes fastened on the hedge opposite, being so intent on what might, perhaps, be described as a visual alibi for Bassett's benefit, in case the lad still happened to be there, that he almost failed to notice that Hartley was busy in his front garden and that Joan was standing by him. He stopped short and bade them "Good-morning."

Mr. Hartley dropped his tools and hastened to the gate. "Good-morning," he said, nervously; "I hope that there is nothing wrong. I went a little way to try and find you."

"Find me?" echoed Mr. Vyner, reddening, as a suspicion of the truth occurred to him.

"Bassett told me that you had been walking up and down waiting to see me," continued Hartley.

"I dressed as fast as I could, but by that time you were out of sight."

Facial contortions, in sympathy with the epithets he was mentally heaping upon the head of Bassett, disturbed for a moment the serenity of Mr. Vyner's countenance. A rapid glance at Miss Hartley helped him to regain his composure.

"I don't know why the boy should have been so officious," he said, slowly; "I didn't want to see you. I certainly passed the house on my way. Oh, yes, and then I thought of going back—I did go a little way back—then I altered my mind again. I suppose I must have passed three times."

"I was afraid there was something wrong," said Hartley. "I am very glad it is all right. I'll give that lad a talking to. He knocked us all up and said that you had been walking up and down for twenty-three minutes."

The generous colour in Mr. Vyner's cheeks was suddenly reflected in Miss Hartley's. Their eyes met, and, feeling exceedingly foolish, he resolved to put a bold face on the matter.

"Bassett is unendurable," he said, with a faint laugh, "and I suspect his watch. Still, I must admit that I did look out for you, because I thought if you were stirring I should like to come in and see what sort of a mess I made last night. Was it very bad?"

"N-no," said Hartley; "no; it perhaps requires a little attention. Half an hour or so will put it right."

"I should like to see my handiwork by daylight," said Robert.

Hartley opened the garden-gate and admitted him, and all three, passing down the garden, stood gravely inspecting the previous night's performance. It is to be recorded to Mr. Vyner's credit that he coughed disparagingly as he eyed it.

"Father says that they only want taking up and replanting," said Joan, softly, "and the footmarks caked over, and the mould cleared away from the path. Except for that your assistance was invaluable."

"I—I didn't quite say that," said Hartley, mildly.

"You ought to have, then," said Robert, severely. "I had no idea it was so bad. You'll have to give me some lessons and see whether I do better next time. Or perhaps Miss Hartley will; she seems to be all right, so far as the theory of the thing goes."

Hartley smiled uneasily, and to avoid replying, moved off a little way and became busy over a rosebush.

"Will you?" inquired Mr. Vyner, very softly. "I believe that I could learn better from you than from anybody; I should take more interest in the work. One wants sympathy from a teacher."

Miss Hartley shook her head. "You had better try a three months' course at Dale's Nurseries," she said, with a smile. "You would get more sympathy from them than from me."

"I would sooner learn from you," persisted Robert.

"I could teach you all I know in half an hour," said the girl.

Mr. Vyner drew a little nearer to her. "You overestimate my powers," he said, in a low voice. "You have no idea how dull I can be; I am sure it would take at least six months."

"That settles it, then," said Joan. "I shouldn't like a dull pupil."

Mr. Vyner drew a little nearer still. "Perhaps—perhaps 'dull' isn't quite the word," he said, musingly.

"It's not the word I should—" began Joan, and stopped suddenly.

"Thank you," murmured Mr. Vyner. "It's nice to be understood. What word would you use?"

Miss Hartley, apparently interested in her father's movements, made no reply.

"Painstaking?" suggested Mr. Vyner; "assiduous? attentive? devoted?"

Miss Hartley, walking toward the house, affected not to hear. 'A fragrant smell of coffee, delicately blended with odour of grilled bacon, came from the open door and turned his thoughts to more mundane things. Mr. Hartley joined them just as the figure of Rosa appeared at the door. "Breakfast is quite ready, miss," she announced.

She stood looking at them, and Mr. Vyner noticed an odd, strained appearance about her left eye which he attributed to a cast. A closer inspection made him almost certain that she was doing her best to wink.

"I laid for three, miss," she said, with great simplicity. "You didn't say whether the gentleman was going to stop or not; and there's no harm done if he don't."

Mr. Hartley started, and in a confused fashion murmured something that sounded like an invitation; Mr. Vyner, in return murmuring something about "goodness" and "not troubling them," promptly followed Joan through the French windows of the small dining-room.

"It's awfully kind of you," he said, heartily, as he seated himself opposite his host; "as a matter of fact I'm half famished."

He made a breakfast which bore ample witness to the truth of his statement; a meal with long intervals of conversation. To Hartley, who usually breakfasted in a quarter of an hour, and was anxious to start for the office, it became tedious in the extreme, and his eyes repeatedly sought the clock. He almost sighed with relief as the visitor took the last piece of toast in the rack, only to be plunged again into depression as his daughter rang the bell for more. Unable to endure it any longer he rose and, murmuring something about getting ready, quitted the room.

"I'm afraid I'm delaying things," remarked Mr. Vyner, looking after him apologetically.

Miss Hartley said, "Not at all," and, as a mere piece of convention, considering that he had already had four cups, offered him some more coffee. To her surprise he at once passed his cup up. She looked at the coffee-pot and for a moment thought enviously of the widow's cruse.

"Only a little, please," he said. "I want it for a toast."

"A toast?" said the girl.

Mr. Vyner nodded mysteriously. "It is a solemn duty," he said, impressively, "and I want you to drink it with me. Are you ready? 'Bassett, the best of boys!'"

Joan Hartley, looking rather puzzled, laughed, and put the cup to her lips. Robert Vyner put his cup down and regarded her intently.

"Do you know why we drank his health?" he inquired.

"No."

"Because," said Robert, pausing for a moment to steady his voice, "because, if it hadn't been for his officiousness, I should not be sitting here with you."

He leaned toward her. "Do you wish that you had not drunk it?" he asked.

Joan Hartley raised her eyes and looked at him so gravely that the mischief, with which he was trying to disguise his nervousness, died out of his face and left it as serious as her own. For a moment her eyes, clear and truthful, met his.

"No," she said, in a low voice.

And at that moment Rosa burst into the room with two pieces of scorched bread and placed them upon the table. Unasked, she proffered evidence on her own behalf, and with great relish divided the blame between the coal merchant, the baker, and the stove. Mr. Hartley entered the room before she had done herself full justice, and Vyner, obeying a glance from Joan, rose to depart.

CHAPTER X

Mr. Vyner spent the remainder of the morning in a state of dreamy exaltation. He leaned back in his chair devising plans for a future in which care and sorrow bore no part, and neglected the pile of work on his table in favour of writing the name "Joan Vyner" on pieces of paper, which he afterward burnt in the grate. At intervals he jumped up and went to the window, in the faint hope that Joan might be passing, and once, in the highest of high spirits, vaulted over his table. Removing ink from his carpet afterward by means of blotting-paper was only an agreeable diversion.

By mid-day his mood had changed to one of extreme tenderness and humility, and he began to entertain unusual misgivings as to his worthiness. He went home to lunch depressed by a sense of his shortcomings; but, on his return, his soaring spirits got the better of him again. Filled with a vast charity, his bosom overflowing with love for all mankind, he looked about to see whom he could benefit; and Bassett entering the room at that moment was sacrificed without delay. Robert Vyner was ashamed to think that he should have left the lad's valuable services unrewarded for so long.

"It's a fine afternoon, Bassett," he said, leaning back and regarding him with a benevolent smile.

"Beautiful, sir," said the youth.

"Too fine to sit in a stuffy office," continued the other. "Put on you hat and go out and enjoy yourself."

"Sir?" said the amazed Bassett.

"Take a half holiday," said Vyner, still smiling.

"Thank you, sir," said Bassett, "but I don't care for holidays; and, besides, I've got a lot of work to do."

"Do it to-morrow," said Vyner. "Go on—out you go!"

"It can't be done to-morrow, sir," said the youth, almost tearfully. "I've got all the letters to copy, and a pile of other work. And besides I shouldn't know what to do with myself if I went."

Mr. Vyner eyed him in astonishment. "I'm sorry to find a tendency to disobedience in you, Bassett," he said, at last. "I've noticed it before. And as to saying that you wouldn't know what to do with yourself, it's a mere idle excuse."

"What time have I got to go, sir?" asked Bassett, resignedly.

"Time?" exclaimed the other. "Now, at once. Avaunt!"

The boy stood for a moment gazing at him in mute appeal, and then, moving with laggard steps to the door, closed it gently behind him. A sudden outbreak of four or five voices, all speaking at once, that filtered through the wall, satisfied Mr. Vyner that his orders were being obeyed.

Horrified at the grave charge of disobedience, Bassett distributed his work and left with what the junior clerk—whom he had constituted residuary legatee—considered unnecessary and indecent haste. The latter gentleman, indeed, to the youth's discomfiture, accompanied him as far as the entrance, and spoke eloquently upon the subject all the way downstairs. His peroration consisted almost entirely of a repetition of the words "lazy fat-head."

With this hostile voice still ringing in his ears Bas-sett strolled aimlessly about the streets of his native town. He spent some time at a stall in front of a second-hand bookshop, and was just deep in an enthralling romance, entitled "Story of a Lump of Coal," when a huge hand was laid upon his shoulder, and he turned to meet the admiring gaze of Mr. Walters.

"More book-larning," said the boatswain, in tones of deep respect. "It's a wonder to me that that head of yours don't bust."

"Heads don't burst," said Bassett. "The brain enlarges with use the same as muscles with exercise. They can't burst."

"I only wish I had arf your laming," said Mr. Walters; "just arf, and I should be a very different man to wot I am now. Well, so long."

"Where are you going?" inquired the youth, replacing the book.

"Seven Trees," replied the other, displaying a small parcel. "I've got to take this over there for the skipper. How far do you make it?"

"Four miles," said Bassett. "I'll come with you, if you like."

"Wot about the office?" inquired the boatswain, in surprise.

Bassett, explained, and a troubled expression appeared on the seaman's face as he listened. He was thinking of the last conversation he had had with the youth, and the hearty way in which he had agreed with him as to the pernicious action of malt and other agreeable liquors on the human frame. He remembered that he had committed himself to the statement that wild horses could not make him drink before six in the evening, and then not more than one half-pint.

"It's a long walk for a 'ot day," he said, slowly. "It might be too much for you."

"Oh, no; I'm a good walker," said Bassett.

"Might be too much for that head of yours," said Mr. Walters, considerately.

"I often walk farther than that," was the reply.

Mr. Walters drew the back of his hand across a mouth which was already dry, and resigned himself to his fate. He had lied quite voluntarily, and pride told him that he must abide by the consequences. And eight miles of dusty road lay between him and relief. He strode along stoutly, and tried to turn an attentive ear to a dissertation on field-mice. At the end of the first mile he saw the sign of the Fox and Hounds peeping through the trees, and almost unconsciously slackened his pace as he remembered that it was the last inn on the road to Seven Trees.

"It's very 'ot," he murmured, mopping his brow with his sleeve, "and I'm as dry as a bone."

"I'm thirsty, too," said Bassett; "but you know the cure for it, don't you?"

"O' course I do," said the boatswain, and nearly smacked his lips.

"Soldiers do it on the march," said Bassett.

"I've seen 'em," said Mr. Walters, grinning.

"A leaden bullet is the best thing," said Bassett, stooping and picking up a pebble, which he polished on his trousers, "but this will do as well. Suck that and you won't be troubled with thirst."

The boatswain took it mechanically, and, after giving it another wipe on his own trousers, placed it with great care in his mouth. Bassett found another pebble and they marched on sucking.

"My thirst has quite disappeared," he said, presently. "How's yours?"

"Worse and worse," said Mr. Walters, gruffly.

"It'll be all right in a minute," said Bassett. "Perhaps I had the best pebble. If it isn't, perhaps we could get a glass of water at a cottage; although it isn't good to drink when you are heated."

Mr. Walters made no reply, but marched on, marvelling at his lack of moral courage. Bassett, quite refreshed, took out his pebble, and after a grateful tribute to its properties placed it in his waistcoat pocket for future emergencies.

By the time they had reached Seven Trees and delivered the parcel Mr. Walters was desperate. The flattering comments that Bassett had made upon his common-sense and virtue were forgotten. Pleading fatigue he sat down by the roadside and, with his eyes glued to the open door of the Pedlar's Rest, began to hatch schemes of deliverance.

A faint smell of beer and sawdust, perceptible even at that distance, set his nostrils aquiver. Then he saw an old labourer walk from the bar to a table, bearing a mug of foaming ale. Human nature could endure no more, and he was just about to throw away a hard-earned character for truth and sobriety when better thoughts intervened. With his eyes fixed on the small figure by his side, he furtively removed the pebble from his mouth, and then with a wild cry threw out his arms and clutched at his throat.

"What's the matter?" cried Bassett, as the boatswain sprang to his feet.

"The stone," cried Mr. Walters, in a strangulated voice; "it's stuck in my throat."

Bassett thumped him on the back like one possessed. "Cough it up!" he cried. "Put your finger down! Cough!"

The boatswain waved his arms and gurgled. "I'm choking!" he moaned, and dashed blindly into the inn, followed by the alarmed boy.

"Pot—six ale!" he gasped, banging on the little counter.

The landlord eyed him in speechless amazement.

"Six ale!" repeated the boatswain. "Pot! Quick! G-r-r."

"You be off," said the landlord, putting down a glass he was wiping, and eying him wrathfully. "How dare you come into my place like that? What do you mean by it?"

"He has swallowed a pebble!" said Bassett, hastily.

"If he'd swallowed a brick I shouldn't be surprised," said the landlord, "seeing the state he's in. I don't want drunken sailors in my place; and, what's more, I won't have 'em."

"Drunk?" said the unfortunate boatswain, raising his voice. "Me? Why, I ain't—"

"Out you go!" said the landlord, in a peremptory voice, "and be quick about it; I don't want people to say you got it here."

"Got it?" wailed Mr. Walters. "Got it? I tell you I ain't had it. I swallowed a stone."

"If you don't go out," said the landlord, as Mr. Walters, in token of good faith, stood making weird noises in his throat and rolling his eyes, "I'll have you put out. How dare you make them noises in my bar! Will—you—go?"

Mr. Walters looked at him, looked at the polished nickel taps, and the neat row of mugs on the shelves. Then, without a word, he turned and walked out.

"Has it gone down?" inquired Bassett presently, as they walked along.

"Wot?" said the boatswain, thoughtlessly.

"The pebble."

"I s'pose so," said the other, sourly.

"I should think it would be all right, then," said the boy; "foreign bodies, even of considerable size, are often swallowed with impunity. How is your thirst now?"

The boatswain stopped dead in the middle of the road and stood eying him suspiciously, but the mild eyes behind the glasses only betrayed friendly solicitude. He grunted and walked on.

By the time the Fox and Hounds came in sight again he had resolved not to lose a reputation which entailed suffering. He clapped the boy on the back, and after referring to a clasp-knive which he remembered to have left on the grass opposite the Pedlar's Rest, announced his intention of going back for it. He did go back as far as a bend in the road, and, after watching Bassett out of sight, hastened with expectant steps into the inn.

He rested there for an hour, and, much refreshed, walked slowly into Salthaven. It was past seven o'clock, and somewhat at a loss how to spend the evening he was bending his steps toward the Lobster Pot, a small inn by the quay, when in turning a corner he came into violent collision with a fashionably attired lady.

"I beg pardon, ma'am," he stammered. "I'm very sorry. I didn't see where I was—Why! Halloa, yaller wig!"

Miss Jelks drew back and, rubbing, her arm, eyed him haughtily.

"Fancy you in a 'at like that," pursued the astonished boatswain. "No wonder I thought you was a lady. Well, and 'ow are you?"

"My health is very well, I thank you," returned Miss Jelks, stiffly.

"That's right," said the boatswain, heartily.

Conversation came suddenly to a standstill, and they stood eying each other awkwardly.

"It's a fine evening," said Mr. Walters, at last.

"Beautiful," said Rosa.

They eyed each other again, thoughtfully.

"You hurt my arm just now," said Rosa, rubbing it coquettishly. "You're very strong, aren't you?"

"Middling," said the boatswain.

"Very strong, I should say," said Rosa. "You've got such a broad chest and shoulders."

The boatswain inflated himself.

"And arms," continued Miss Jelks, admiringly. "Arms like—like—"

"Blocks o' wood," suggested the modest Mr. Walters, squinting at them complacently.

"Or iron," said Rosa. "Well, good-by; it's my evening out, and I mustn't waste it."

"Where are you going?" inquired the boatswain.

Miss Jelks shook her head. "I don't know," she said, softly.

"You can come with me if you like," said Mr. Walters, weighing his words carefully. "A little way. I ain't got nothing better to do."

Miss Jelks's eyes flashed, then with a demure smile she turned and walked by his side. They walked slowly up the street, and Mr. Walters's brows grew black as a series of troublesome coughs broke out behind. A glance over his shoulder showed him three tavern acquaintances roguishly shaking their heads at him.

"Arf a second," he said, stopping. "I'll give 'em something to cough about."

Rosa clutched his arm. "Not now; not while you are with me," she said, primly.

"Just one smack," urged the boatswain.

He looked round again and clenched his fists, as his friends, with their arms fondly encircling each other's waists, walked mincingly across the road. He shook off the girl's arm and stepped off the pavement as with little squeals, fondly believed to be feminine, they sought sanctuary in the Red Lion.

"They're not worth taking notice of," said Rosa.

She put a detaining hand through his arm again and gave it a little gentle squeeze. A huge feather almost rested on his shoulder, and the scent of eau-de-Cologne assailed his nostrils. He walked on in silent amazement at finding himself in such a position.

"It's nice to be out," said Rosa, ignoring a feeble attempt on his part to release his arm. "You've no idea how fresh the air smells after you've been shut up all day."

"You've got a comfortable berth, though, haven't you?" said Mr. Walters.

"Fairish," said Rosa. "There's plenty of work; but I like work—housework."

The boatswain said "Oh!"

"Some girls can't bear it," said Rosa, "but then, as I often say, what are they going to do when they get married?"

"Ah!" said the boatswain, with an alarmed grunt, and made another attempt to release his arm.

"Oh, I beg your pardon," said Rosa, making a pretence of freeing him. "I'm afraid I'm leaning on you; but I sprained my ankle yesterday, and I thought—"

"All right," said Mr. Walters, gruffly.

"Thank you," said Rosa, and leaned on him heavily. "Housework is the proper thing for girls," she continued, with some severity. "Every girl ought to know how to keep her husband's house clean and cook nicely for him. But there—all they think about is love. What did you say?"

"Nothing," said Mr. Walters, hastily. "I didn't say a word."

"I don't understand it myself," said Rosa, takings an appraising glance at him from under the brim of her hat; "I can't think why people want to get married when they're comfortable."

"Me neither," said the boatswain.

"Being friends is all right," said Rosa, meditatively, "but falling in love and getting married always seemed absurd to me."

"Me too," said Mr. Walters, heartily.

With a mind suddenly at ease he gave himself over to calm enjoyment of the situation. He sniffed approvingly at the eau-de-Cologne, and leaned heavily toward the feather. Apparently without either of them knowing it, his arm began to afford support to Miss Jelks's waist. They walked on for a long time in silence.

"Some men haven't got your sense," said Rosa, at last, with a sigh. "There's a young fellow that brings the milk—nice young fellow I thought he was—and all because I've had a word with him now and again, he tried to make love to me."

"Oh, did he?" said Mr. Walters, grimly. "What's his name?"

"It don't matter," said Rosa. "I don't think he'll try it again."

"Still, I might as well learn 'im a lesson," said the boatswain. "I like a bit of a scrap."

"If you are going to fight everybody that tries to take notice of me you'll have your work cut out," said Miss Jelks, in tones of melancholy resignation, "and I'm sure it's not because I give them any encouragement. And as for the number that ask me to walk out with them—well, there!"

Mr. Walters showed his sympathy with such a state of affairs by a pressure that nearly took her breath away. They sat for an hour and a half on a bench by the river discussing the foolishness of young men.

"If any of them chaps trouble you again," he said, as they shook hands at the gate of Laurel Lodge, "you let me know. Do you have Sunday evening out too?"

CHAPTER XI

"I have been knocking for the last ten minutes," said Hartley, as he stood one evening at the open door of No. 5, Tranquil Vale, and looked up at Captain Trimblett.

"I was in the summer-house," said the captain, standing aside to let him enter.

"Alone?" queried the visitor.

"Alone? Yes, of course," said the captain, sharply. "Why shouldn't I be? Peter's courting—as usual."

"And Mrs. Chinnery?" inquired the other.

"She's away for a day or two," replied the captain; "friends at Marsham."

He stopped in the small kitchen to get some beer and glasses, and, with the bottle gripped under his arm and a glass in each hand, led the way to the summer-house.

"I came to ask your advice," said Hartley, as he slowly filled his pipe from the pouch the captain pushed toward him.

"Joan?" inquired the captain, who was carefully decanting the beer.

Mr. Hartley nodded.

"Robert Vyner?" pursued the captain.

Hartley nodded again.

"What did I tell you?" inquired the other, placing a full tumbler before him. "I warned you from the first. I told you how it would be. I—"

"It's no good talking like that," said Hartley, with feeble irritation. "You're as bad as my poor old grandmother; she always knew everything before it happened—at least, she said so afterward. What I want to know is: how is it to be stopped? He has been round three nights running."

"Your grandmother is dead, I suppose?" said the offended captain, gazing at the river. "Else she might have known what to do."

"I'm sorry," said Hartley, apologetically; "but I am so worried that I hardly know what I'm saying."

"That's all right," said the captain, amiably. He drank some beer and, leaning back on the seat, knitted his brows thoughtfully.

"He admired her from the first," he said, slowly. "I saw that. Does she like him, I wonder?"

"It looks like it," was the reply.

The captain shook his head. "They'd make a fine couple," he said, slowly. "As fine as you'd see anywhere. It's fate again. Perhaps he was meant to admire her; perhaps millions of years ago—"

"Yes, yes, I know," said Hartley, hastily; "but to prevent it."

"Fate can't be prevented," said the captain, who was now on his favourite theme. "Think of the millions of things that had to happen to make it possible for those two young people to meet and cause this trouble. That's what I mean. If only one little thing had been missing, one little circumstance out of millions, Joan wouldn't have been born; you wouldn't have been born."

Mr. Hartley attempted to speak, but the captain, laying down his pipe, extended an admonitory finger.

"To go back only a little way," he said, solemnly, "your father had the measles, hadn't he?"

"I don't know—I believe so," said Hartley.

"Good," said the captain; "and he pulled through 'em, else you wouldn't have been here. Again, he happened to go up North to see a friend who was taken ill while on a journey, and met your mother there, didn't he?"

Hartley groaned.

"If your father's friend hadn't been taken ill," said the captain, with tremendous solemnity, as he laid his forefinger on his friend's knee, "where would you have been?"

"I don't know," said Hartley, restlessly, "and I don't care."

"Nobody knows," said the other, shaking his head. "The thing is, as you are here, it seems to me that things couldn't have been otherwise. They were all arranged. When your father went up North in that light-hearted fashion, I don't suppose he thought for a moment that you'd be sitting here to-day worrying over one of the results of his journey."

"Of course he didn't," exclaimed Hartley, impatiently; "how could he? Look here, Trimblett, when you talk like that I don't know where I am. If my father hadn't married my mother I suppose he would have married somebody else."

"My idea is that he couldn't," said the captain, obstinately. "If a thing has got to be it will be, and there's no good worrying about it. Take a simple example. Some time you are going to die of a certain disease—you can only die once—and you're going to be buried in a certain grave—you can only be buried in one grave. Try and think that in front of you there is that one particular disease told off to kill you at a certain date, and in one particular spot of all this earth there is a grave waiting to be dug for you. At present we don't know the date, or the disease, or the grave, but there they are, all waiting for you. That is fate. What is the matter? Where are you going?"

"Home," said Hartley, bitterly, as he paused at the door. "I came round to you for a little help, and you go on in a way that makes my flesh creep. Good-by."

"Wait a bit," said the captain, detaining him. "Wait a bit; let's see what can be done."

He pulled the other back into his seat again and, fetching another bottle of beer from the house to stimulate invention, sat evolving schemes for his friend's relief, the nature of which reflected more credit upon his ingenuity than his wisdom.

"But, after all," he said, as Hartley made a third attempt to depart, "what is the good? The very steps we take to avoid disaster may be the ones to bring it on. While you are round here getting advice from me, Robert Vyner may be availing himself of the opportunity to propose."

Hartley made no reply. He went out and walked' up and down the garden, inspecting it. The captain, who was no gardener, hoped that the expression of his face was due to his opinion of the flowers.

"You must miss Mrs. Chinnery," said Hartley, at last.

"No," said the captain, almost explosively; "not at all. Why should I?"

"It can't be so homelike without her," said Hartley, stooping to pull up a weed or two.

"Just the same," said the other, emphatically. "We have a woman in to do the work, and it doesn't make the slightest difference to me—not the slightest."

"How is Truefitt?" inquired Hartley.

The captain's face darkened. "Peter's all right," he said, slowly. "He's not treated me—quite well," he added, after a little hesitation.

"It's natural he should neglect you a bit, as things are," said his friend.

"Neglect?" said the captain, bitterly. "I wish he would neglect me. He's turning out a perfect busybody, and he's getting as artful as they make 'em. I never would have believed it of Peter. Never."

Hartley waited.

"I met Cap'n Walsh the other night," said Trimblett; "we hadn't seen each other for years, and we went into the Golden Fleece to have a drink. You know what Walsh is when he's ashore. And he's a man that won't be beaten. He had had four tries to get a 'cocktail' right that he had tasted in New York, and while he was superintending the mixing of the fifth I slipped out. The others were all right as far as I could judge; but that's Walsh all over."

"Well?" said Hartley.

"I came home and found Peter sitting all alone in the dumps," continued the captain. "He has been very down of late, and, what was worse, he had got a bottle of whiskey on the table. That's a fatal thing to begin; and partly to keep him company, but mainly to prevent him drinking more than was good for him, I helped him finish the bottle—there wasn't much in it."

"Well?" said Hartley again, as the captain paused.

"He got talking about his troubles," said the captain, slowly. "You know how things are, and, like a fool, I tried to cheer him up by agreeing with him that Mrs. Chinnery would very likely make things easy for him by marrying again. In fact, so far as I remember, I even helped him to think of the names of one or two likely men. He said she'd make anybody as good a wife as a man could wish."

"So she would," said Hartley, looking at him with sudden interest. "In fact, I have often wondered—"

"He went on talking like that," continued the captain, hastily, "and out of politeness and good feeling I agreed with him. What else could I do? Then—I didn't take much notice of it because, as I said, he was drinking whiskey—he—he sort of wondered why—why—"

"Why you didn't offer to marry her?" interrupted Hartley.

The captain nodded. "It took my breath away," he said, impressively, "and I lost my presence of mind. Instead of speaking out plain I tried to laugh it off—just to spare his feelings—and said I wasn't worthy of her."

"What did he say?" inquired Hartley, curiously, after another long pause.

"Nothing," replied the captain. "Not a single word. He just gave me a strange look, shook my hand hard, and went off to bed. I've been uneasy in my mind ever since. I hardly slept a wink last night; and Peter behaves as though there is some mysterious secret between us. What would you do?"

Mr. Hartley took his friend's arm and paced thoughtfully up and down the garden.

"Why not marry her?" he said, at last.

"Because I don't want to," said the captain, almost violently.

"You'd be safer at sea, then," said the other.

"The ship won't be ready for sea for weeks yet," said Captain Trimblett, dolefully. "She's going on a time-charter, and before she is taken over she has got to be thoroughly overhauled. As fast as they put one thing right something else is found to be wrong."

"Go to London and stay with your children for a bit, then," said Hartley. "Give out that you are only going for a day or two, and then don't turn up till the ship sails."

The captain's face brightened. "I believe Vyner would let me go," he replied. "I could go in a few days' time, at any rate. And, by the way—Joan!"

"Eh?" said Hartley.

"Write to your brother-in-law at Highgate, and send her there for a time," said the captain. "Write and ask him to invite her. Keep her and young Vyner apart before things go too far."

"I'll see how things go for a bit," said Hartley, slowly. "It's awkward to write and ask for an invitation. And where do your ideas of fate come in?" "They come in all the time," said the captain, with great seriousness. "Very likely my difficulty was made on purpose for us to think of a way of getting you out of yours. Or it might be Joan's fate to meet somebody in London at her uncle's and marry him. If she goes we might arrange to go up together, so that I could look after her."

"I'll think it over," said his friend, holding out his hand. "I must be going."

"I'll come a little way with you," said the captain, leading the way into the house. "I don't suppose Peter will be in yet, but he might; and I've had more of him lately than I want."

He took up his hat and, opening the door, followed Hartley out into the road. The evening was warm, and they walked slowly, the captain still discoursing on fate and citing various instances of its working which had come under his own observation. He mentioned, among others, the case of a mate of his who found a wife by losing a leg, the unfortunate seaman falling an easy victim to the nurse who attended him.

"He always put it down to the effects of the chloroform," concluded the captain; "but my opinion is, it was to be."

He paused at Hartley's gate, and was just indulging in the usual argument as to whether he should go indoors for a minute or not, when a man holding a handkerchief to his bleeding face appeared suddenly round the corner of the house and, making a wild dash for the gate, nearly overturned the owner.

"It looks like our milkman!" said Hartley, recovering his balance and gazing in astonishment after the swiftly retreating figure. "I wonder what was the matter with him?"

"He would soon know what was the matter with him if I got hold of him," said the wrathful captain.

Hartley opened the door with his key, and the captain, still muttering under his breath, passed in. Rosa's voice, raised in expostulation, sounded loudly from the kitchen, and a man's voice, also raised, was heard in response.

"Sounds like my bo'sun," said the captain, staring as he passed into the front room. "What's he doing here?"

Hartley shook his head.

"Seems to be making himself at home," said the captain, fidgeting. "He's as noisy as if he was in his own house."

"I don't suppose he knows you are here," said his friend, mildly.

Captain Trimblett still fidgeted. "Well, it's your house," he said at last. "If you don't mind that lanky son of a gun making free, I suppose it's no business of mine. If he made that noise aboard my ship—"

Red of face he marched to the window and stood looking out. Fortified by his presence, Hartley rang the bell.

"Is there anybody in the kitchen?" he inquired, as Rosa answered it. "I fancied I heard a man's voice."

"The milkman was here just now," said Rosa, and, eying him calmly, departed.

The captain swung round in wrathful amazement.

"By—," he spluttered; "I've seen—well—by—b-r-r-r—Can I ring for that damned bo'sun o' mine?

"Certainly," said Hartley.

The captain crossed to the fireplace and, seizing the bell-handle, gave a pull that made the kitchen resound with wild music. After a decent interval, apparently devoted to the allaying of masculine fears, Rosa appeared again.

"Did you ring, sir?" she inquired, gazing at her master.

"Send that bo'sun o' mine here at once!" said the captain, gruffly.

Rosa permitted herself a slight expression of surprise. "Bo'sun, sir?" she asked, politely.

"Yes."

The girl affected to think. "Oh, you mean Mr. Walters?" she said, at last.

"Send him here," said the captain.

Rosa retired slowly, and shortly afterward something was heard brushing softly against the wall of the passage. It ceased for a time, and just as the captain's patience was nearly at an end there was a sharp exclamation, and Mr. Walters burst suddenly into the room and looked threateningly over his shoulder at somebody in the passage.

"What are you doing here?" demanded Captain Trimblett, loudly.

Mr. Walters eyed him uneasily, and with his cap firmly gripped in his left hand saluted him with the right. Then he turned his head sideways toward the passage. The captain repeated his question in a voice, if anything, louder than before.

The strained appearance of Mr. Walters's countenance relaxed.

"Come here for my baccy-box, wot I left here the other day," he said, glibly, "when you sent me."

"What were you making that infernal row about, then?" demanded the captain.

Mr. Walters cast an appealing glance toward the passage and listened acutely. "I was—grumbling because—I couldn't—find it," he said, with painstaking precision.

"Grumbling?" repeated the captain. "That ugly voice of yours was enough to bring the ceiling down. What was the matter with that man that burst out of the gate as we came in, eh?"

The boatswain's face took on a wooden expression.

"He—his nose was bleeding," he said, at last.

"I know that," said the captain, grimly; "but what made it bleed?"

For a moment Mr. Walters looked like a man who has been given a riddle too difficult for human solution. Then his face cleared again.

"He—he told me—he was object—subject to it," he stammered. "Been like it since he was a baby."

He shifted his weight to his other foot and shrugged eloquently the shoulder near the passage.

"What did you do to him?" demanded the captain, in a low, stern voice.

"Me, sir?" said Mr. Walters, with clumsy surprise. "Me, sir? I—I—all I done—all I done—was ta put a door-key down his back."

"Door-key?" roared the captain.

"To—to stop the bleeding, sir," said Mr. Walters, looking at the floor and nervously twisting his cap in his hands. "It's a old-fashioned—"

"That'll do," exclaimed the captain, in a choking voice, "that'll do. I don't want any more of your lies. How dare you come to Mr. Hartley's house and knock his milkman about, eh? How dare you? What do you mean by it?"

Mr. Walters fumbled with his cap again. "I was sitting in the kitchen," he said at last, "sitting in the kitchen—hunting 'igh and low for my baccy-box—when this 'ere miserable, insulting chap shoves his head in at the door and calls the young lady names."

"Names?" said the captain, frowning, and waving an interruption from Hartley aside. "What names?"

Mr. Walters hesitated again, and his brow grew almost as black as the captain's.

"'Rosy-lips,'" he said, at last; "and I give 'im such a wipe acrost—"

"Out you go," cried the wrathful captain. "Out you go, and if I hear your pretty little voice in this house again you'll remember it, I can tell you. D'ye hear? Scoot!"

Mr. Walters said "Thank you," and, retiring with an air of great deference, closed the door softly behind him.

"There's another of them," said Captain Trimblett subsiding into a chair. "And from little things I had heard here and there I thought he regarded women as poison. Fate again, I suppose; he was made to regard them as poison all these years for the sake of being caught by that tow-headed wench in your kitchen."

CHAPTER XII

By no means insensible to the difficulties in the way, Joan Hartley had given no encouragement to Mr. Robert Vyner to follow up the advantage afforded him by her admission at the breakfast-table. Her father's uneasiness, coupled with the broad hints which Captain Trimblett mistook for tactfulness, only confirmed her in her resolution; and Mr. Vyner, in his calmer moments, had to admit to himself that she was right—for the present, at any rate. Meantime, they were both young, and, with the confidence of youth, he looked forward to a future in which his father's well-known views on social distinctions and fitting matrimonial alliances should have undergone a complete change. As to his mother, she merely seconded his father's opinions, and, with admiration born of love and her marriage vows, filed them for reference in a memory which had on more than one occasion been a source of great embarrassment to a man who had not lived for over fifty years without changing some of them.

Deeply conscious of his own moderation, it was, therefore, with a sense of annoyance that Mr. Robert Vyner discovered that Captain Trimblett was actually attempting to tackle him upon the subject which he considered least suitable for discussion. They were sitting in his office, and the captain, in pursuit of a promise to Hartley, after two or three references to the weather, and a long account of an uninteresting conversation with a policeman, began to get on to dangerous ground.

"I've been in the firm's service a good many years now," he began.

"I hope you'll be in as many more," said Vyner, regarding him almost affectionately.

"Hartley has been with you a long time, too," continued Trimblett, slowly. "We became chums the first time we met, and we've been friends ever since. Not just fair-weather friends, but close and hearty; else I wouldn't venture to speak to you as I'm going to speak."

Mr. Vyner looked up at him suddenly, his face hard and forbidding. Then, as he saw the embarrassment in the kindly old face before him, his anger vanished and he bent his head to hide a smile.

"Fire away," he said, cordially.

"I'm an old man," began the captain, solemnly.

"Nonsense," interrupted Robert, breezily. "Old man indeed! A man is as old as he feels, and I saw you the other night, outside the Golden Fleece, with Captain Walsh—"

"I couldn't get away from him," said the captain, hastily.

"So far as I could see you were not trying," continued the remorseless Robert. "You were instructing him in the more difficult and subtle movements of a hornpipe, and I must say I thought your elasticity was wonderful—wonderful."

"It was just the result of an argument I had with him," said the captain, looking very confused, "and I ought to have known better. But, as I was saying, I am an old man, and—"

"But you look so young," protested Mr. Vyner.

"Old man," repeated the captain, ignoring the remark. "Old age has its privileges, and one of them is to give a word in season before it is too late."

"'A stitch in time saves nine," quoted Robert, with an encouraging nod.

"And I was speaking to Hartley the other day," continued the captain. "He hasn't been looking very well of late, and, as far as I can make out, he is a little bit worried over the matter I want to speak to you about."

Robert Vyner's face hardened again for a moment. He leaned back in his chair and, playing with his watch-chain, regarded the other intently. Then he smiled maliciously.

"He told me," he said, nodding.

"Told you?" repeated the captain, in astonishment.

Mr. Vyner nodded again, and bending down pretended to glance at some papers on his table.

"Green-fly," he said, gravely. "He told me that he syringes early and late. He will clear a tree, as he thinks, and while he has gone to mix another bucket of the stuff there are several generations born.

Bassett informs me that a green-fly is a grandfather before it is half an hour old. So you see it is hopeless. Quite."

Captain Trimblett listened with ill-concealed impatience. "I was thinking of something more important than green-flies," he said, emphatically.

"Yes?" said Vyner, thoughtfully.

It was evident that the old sailor was impervious to hints. Rendered unscrupulous by the other's interference, and at the same time unwilling to hurt his feelings, Mr. Vyner bethought himself of a tale to which he had turned an unbelieving ear only an hour or two before.

"Of course, I quite forgot," he said, apologetically. "How stupid of me! I hope that you'll accept my warmest congratulations and be very, very happy. I can't tell you how pleased I am. But for the life of me I can't see why it should worry Hartley."

"Congratulations?" said the captain, eying him in surprise. "What about?"

"Your marriage," replied Robert. "I only heard of it on my way to the office, and your talking put it out of my head."

"Me?" said Captain Trimblett, going purple with suppressed emotion. "My marriage? I'm not going to be married. Not at all."

"What do you mean by 'not at all?'" inquired Mr. Vyner, looking puzzled. "It isn't a thing you can do by halves."

"I'm not going to be married at all," said the captain, raising his voice. "I never thought of such a thing. Who—who told you?"

"A little bird," said Robert, with a simpering air.

Captain Trimblett took out a handkerchief, and after blowing his nose violently and wiping his heated face expressed an overpowering desire to wring the little bird's neck.

"Who was it?" he repeated.

"A little bird of the name of Sellers—Captain Sellers," replied Robert. "I met him on my way here, hopping about in the street, simply brimming over with the news."

"There isn't a word of truth in it," said the agitated captain. "I never thought of such a thing. That old mischief-making mummy must be mad—stark, starin' mad."

"Dear me!" said Robert, regretfully. "He seems such a dear old chap, and I thought it was so nice to see a man of his age so keenly interested in the love-affairs of a younger generation. Anybody might have thought you were his own son from the way he talked of you."

"I'll 'son' him!" said the unhappy captain, vaguely.

"He is very deaf," said Robert, gently, "and perhaps he may have misunderstood somebody. Perhaps somebody told him you were not going to be married. Funny he shouts so, isn't it? Most deaf people speak in a very low voice."

"Did he shout that?" inquired Captain Trimblett, in a quivering voice.

"Bawled it," replied Mr. Vyner, cheerfully; "but as it isn't true, I really think that you ought to go and tell Captain Sellers at once. There is no knowing what hopes he may be raising. He is a fine old man; but perhaps, after all, he is a wee bit talkative."

Captain Trimblett, who had risen, stood waiting impatiently until the other had finished, and then, forgetting all about the errand that had brought him there, departed in haste. Mr. Vyner went to the window, and a broad smile lit up his face as he watched the captain hurrying across the bridge. With a blessing on the head of the most notorious old gossip in Salthaven, he returned to his work.

Possessed by a single idea, Captain Trimblett sped on his way at a pace against which both his age and his figure protested in vain. By the time he reached Tranquil Vale he was breathless, and hardly able to gasp his inquiry for Captain Sellers to the old housekeeper who attended the door.

"He's a-sitting in the garden looking at his flowers," she replied. "Will you go through?"

Captain Trimblett went through. His head was erect and his face and eyes blazing. A little old gentleman, endowed with the far sight peculiar to men who have followed the sea, who was sitting in a deck-chair at the bottom of the garden, glimpsed him and at once collapsed. By the time the captain reached the chair he discovered a weasel-faced, shrunken old figure in a snuff-coloured suit of clothes sunk in a profound slumber. He took him by the arms and shook him roughly.

"Yes? Halloa! What's matter?" inquired Captain Sellers, half waking.

Captain Trimblett arched his hand over his mouth and bent to an ear apparently made of yellow parchment.

"Cap'n Sellers," he said, in a stern, thrilling voice, "I've got a bone to pick with you."

The old man opened his eyes wide and sat blinking at him. "I've been asleep," he said, with a senile chuckle. "How do, Cap'n Trimblett?"

"I've got a bone to pick with you," repeated the other.

"Eh?" said Captain Sellers, putting his hand to his ear.

"A—bone—to—pick—with—you," said the incensed Trimblett, raising his voice. "What do you mean by it?"

"Eh?" said Captain Sellers, freshly.

"What do you mean by saying things about me?" bawled Trimblett. "How dare you go spreading false reports about me? I'll have the law of you."

Captain Sellers smiled vaguely and shook his head.

"I'll prosecute you," bellowed Captain Trimblett. "You're shamming, you old fox. You can hear what I say plain enough. You've been spreading reports that I'm going to—"

He stopped and looked round just in time. Attracted by the volume of his voice, the housekeeper had come to the back door, two faces appeared at the next-door windows, and the back of Mr. Peter Truefitt was just disappearing inside his summer-house.

"I know you are talking," said Captain Sellers, plaintively, "because I can see your lips moving. It's a great affliction—deafness."

He fell back in his chair again, and, with a crafty old eye cocked on the windows next door, fingered a scanty tuft of white hair on his chin and smiled weakly. Captain Trimblett controlled himself by an effort, and, selecting a piece of paper from a bundle of letters in his pocket, made signs for a pencil. Captain Sellers shook his head; then he glanced round uneasily as Trimblett, with an exclamation of satisfaction, found an inch in his waistcoat-pocket and began to write. He nodded sternly at the paper when he had finished, and handed it to Captain Sellers.

The old gentleman received it with a pleasant smile, and, extricating himself from his chair in a remarkable fashion considering his age, began to fumble in his pockets. He went through them twice, and his countenance, now lighted by hope and now darkened by despair, conveyed to Captain Trimblett as accurately as speech could have done the feelings of a man to whom all reading matter, without his spectacles, is mere dross.

"I can't find my glasses," said Captain Sellers, at last, lowering himself into the chair. Then he put his hand to his ear and turned toward his visitor. "Try again," he said, encouragingly.

Captain Trimblett eyed him for a moment in helpless wrath, and then, turning on his heel, marched back through the house, and after standing irresolute for a second or two entered his own. The front room was empty, and from the silence he gathered that Mrs. Chinnery was out. He filled his pipe, and throwing himself into an easy-chair sought to calm his nerves with tobacco, while he tried to think out his position. His meditations were interrupted by the entrance of Mr. Truefitt, and something in the furtive way that gentleman eyed him as he came into the room only served to increase his uneasiness.

"Very warm," said Truefitt.

The captain assented, and with his eyes fixed on the mantelpiece smoked in silence.

"I saw you... talking... to Captain Sellers just now," said Mr. Truefitt, after a long pause.

"Aye," said the captain. "You did."

His eyes came from the mantelpiece and fixed themselves on those of his friend. Mr. Truefitt in a flurried fashion struck a match and applied it to his empty pipe.

"I'll have the law of him," said the captain, fiercely; "he has been spreading false reports about me."

"Reports?" repeated Mr. Truefitt, in a husky voice.

"He has been telling everybody that I am about to be married," thundered the captain.

Mr. Truefitt scratched the little bit of gray whisker that grew by his ear.

"I told him," he said at last.

"You?" exclaimed the amazed captain. "But it isn't true."

Mr. Truefitt turned to him with a smile intended to be arch and reassuring. The result, owing to his nervousness, was so hideous that the captain drew back in dismay.

"It's—it's all right," said Mr. Truefitt at last. "Ah! If it hadn't been for me you might have gone on hoping for years and years, without knowing the true state of her feelings toward you."

"What do you mean?" demanded the captain, gripping the arms of his chair.

"Sellers is a little bit premature," said Mr. Truefitt, coughing. "There is nothing settled yet, of course. I told him so. Perhaps I oughtn't to have mentioned it at all just yet, but I was so pleased to find that it was all right I had to tell somebody."

"What are you—talking about?" gasped the captain.

Mr. Truefitt looked up, and by a strong effort managed to meet the burning gaze before him.

"I told Susanna," he said, with a gulp.

"Told her? Told her what?" roared the captain.

"Told her that you said you were not worthy of her," replied Mr. Truefitt, very slowly and distinctly.

The captain took his pipe out of his mouth, and laying it on the table with extreme care listened mechanically while the clock struck five.

"What did she say?" he inquired, hoarsely, after the clock had finished.

Mr. Truefitt leaned over, and with a trembling hand patted him on the shoulder.

"She said, 'Nonsense'" he replied, softly.

The captain rose and, putting on his cap—mostly over one eye—put out his hands like a blind man for the door, and blundered out into the street.

CHAPTER XIII

"Mr. Vyner wants to see you, sir," said Bassett, as Hartley, coming in from a visit to the harbour, hung his hat on a peg and began to change into the old coat he wore in the office. "Mr. John; he has rung three times."

The chief clerk changed his coat again, and after adjusting his hair in the little piece of unframed glass which he had bought in the street for a penny thirty years before, hastened to the senior partner's room.

Mr. Vyner, who was rinsing his hands in a little office washstand that stood in the corner, looked round at his entrance and, after carefully drying his hands on a soft towel, seated himself at his big writing table, and, leaning back, sat thoughtfully regarding his finger-nails. His large, white, freckled hands were redolent of scented soap, and, together with his too regular teeth, his bald head, and white side-whiskers, gave him an appearance of almost aggressive cleanliness.

"I rang for you several times," he said, looking up with a frown.

"I have just come back from Wilson's," said Hartley; "you told me to see them to-day."

Mr. Vyner said "Yes," and, caressing his shaven chin in his hand, appeared to forget the other's existence.

"How long have you been with us?" he inquired at last.

"Thirty-five years, sir," said Hartley, studying his face with sudden anxiety.

"A long time," said the senior partner, dryly. "A long time."

"A pleasant time, sir," ventured the other, in a low voice.

Mr. Vyner's features relaxed, and took on—after some trouble—an appearance of benevolence.

"I hope so," he said, in patronizing tones. "I hope so. Vyner and Son have the name for being good masters. I have never heard any complaints."

He pushed his chair back and, throwing one leg over the other, looked down at his patent-leather boots. The benevolent expression had disappeared.

"Thirty-five years," he said, slowly. "H'm! I had no idea it was so long. You have—ha—no family, worth mentioning?"

"One daughter," said Hartley, his lips going suddenly dry.

"Just so. Just so," said the senior partner. He looked at his boots again. "And she is old enough to earn her own living. Or she might marry. You are in a fortunate position."

Hartley, still watching him anxiously, bowed.

"In the event, for instance," continued Mr. Vyner, in careless tones— "in the event of your retiring from the service of Vyner and Son, there is nobody that would suffer much. That is a great consideration—a very great consideration."

Hartley, unable to speak, bowed again.

"Change," continued Mr. Vyner, with the air of one uttering a new but indisputable fact—"change is good for us all. So long as you retain your present position there is, of course, a little stagnation in the office; the juniors see their way barred."

He took up a paper-knife and, balancing it between his fingers, tapped lightly with it on the table.

"Is your daughter likely to be married soon?" he inquired, looking up suddenly.

Hartley shook his head. "N-no; I don't think so," he said, thickly.

The senior partner resumed his tapping.

"That is a pity," he said at last, with a frown. "Of course, you understand that Vyner and Son are not anxious to dispense with your services—not at all. In certain circumstances you might remain with us another ten or fifteen years, and then go with a good retiring allowance. At your present age there would be no allowance. Do you understand me?"

The chief clerk tried to summon a little courage, little dignity.

"I am afraid I don't," he said, in a low voice. "It is all so sudden. I—I am rather bewildered." Mr. Vyner looked at him impatiently.

He leaned back in his chair, and watched his chief clerk closely

"I said just now," he continued, in a hard voice, "that Vyner and Son are not anxious to dispense with your services. That is, in a way, a figure of speech. Mr. Robert knows nothing of this, and I may tell you—as an old and trusted servant of the firm—that his share as a partner is at present but nominal, and were he to do anything seriously opposed to my wishes, such as, for instance—such as a—ha—matrimonial alliance of which I could not approve, the results for him would be disastrous. Do you understand?"

In a slow, troubled fashion Hartley intimated that he did. He began to enter into explanations, and was stopped by the senior partner's uplifted hand.

"That will do," said the latter, stiffly. "I have no doubt I know all that you could tell me. It is—ha—only out of consideration for your long and faithful service that I have—ha—permitted you a glimpse into my affairs—our affairs. I hope, now, that I have made myself quite clear."

He leaned back in his chair and, twisting the paper-knife idly between his fingers, watched his chief clerk closely.

"Wouldn't it be advisable—" began Hartley, and stopped abruptly at the expression on the other's face. "I was thinking that if you mentioned this to Mr. Robert—"

"Certainly not!" said Mr. Vyner, with great sharpness. "Certainly not!"

Anger at having to explain affairs to his clerk, and the task of selecting words which should cause the least loss of dignity, almost deprived him of utterance.

"This is a private matter," he said at last, "strictly between ourselves. I am master here, and any alteration in the staff is a matter for myself alone. I do not wish—in fact, I forbid you to mention the matter to him. Unfortunately, we do not always see eye to eye. He is young, and perhaps hardly as worldly wise as I could wish."

He leaned forward to replace the paper-knife on the table, and, after blowing his nose with some emphasis, put the handkerchief back in his pocket and sat listening with a judicial air for anything that his chief clerk might wish to put before him.

"It would be a great blow to me to leave the firm," said Hartley, after two ineffectual attempts to speak. "I have been in it all my life—all my life. At my age I could scarcely hope to get any other employment worth having. I have always tried to do my best. I have never—"

"Yes, yes," said the other, interrupting with a wave of his hand; "that has been recognized. Your remuneration has, I believe, been in accordance with your—ha—services. And I suppose you have made some provision?"

Hartley shook his head. "Very little," he said, slowly. "My wife was ill for years before she died, and I have had other expenses. My life is insured, so that in case of anything happening to me there would be something for my daughter, but that is about all."

"And in case of dismissal," said the senior partner, with some cheerfulness, "the insurance premium would, of course, only be an extra responsibility. It is your business, of course; but if I were—ha—in your place I should—ha—marry my daughter off as soon as possible. If you could come to me in three months and tell me—"

He broke off abruptly and, sitting upright, eyed his clerk steadily.

"That is all, I think," he said at last. "Oh, no mention of this, of course, in the office—I have no desire to raise hopes of promotion in the staff that may not be justified; I may say that I hope will not be justified."

He drew his chair to the table, and with a nod of dismissal took up his pen. Hartley went back to his work with his head in a whirl, and for the first time in twenty years cast a column of figures incorrectly, thereby putting a great strain on the diplomacy of the junior who made the discovery.

He left at his usual hour, and, free from the bustle of the office, tried to realize the full meaning of his interview with Mr. Vyner. He thought of his pleasant house and garden, and the absence of demand in Salthaven for dismissed clerks of over fifty. His thoughts turned to London, but he had grown up with Vyner and Son and had but little to sell in the open market. Walking with bent head he cannoned against a passer-by, and, looking up to apologize, caught sight of Captain Trimblett across the way, standing in front of a jeweller's window.

A tall, sinewy man in a serge suit, whom Hartley recognized as Captain Walsh, was standing by him. His attitude was that of an indulgent policeman with a refractory prisoner, and twice Hartley saw him lay hold of the captain by the coat-sleeve, and call his attention to something in the window. Anxious to discuss his affairs with Trimblett, Hartley crossed the road.

"Ah! here's Hartley," said the tall captain, with an air of relief, as Captain Trimblett turned and revealed a hot face mottled and streaked with red. "Make him listen to reason. He won't do it for me.

"What's the matter?" inquired Hartley, listlessly.

"A friend o' mine," said Captain Walsh, favouring him with a hideous wink, "a great friend o' mine, is going to be married, and I want to give him a wedding present before I go. I sail to-morrow."

"Well, ask him what he'd like," said Trimblett, making another ineffectual attempt to escape. "Don't bother me."

"I can't do that," said Walsh, with another wink; "it's awkward; besides which, his modesty, would probably make him swear that he wasn't going to be married at all. In fact, he has told me that already. I want you to choose for him. Tell me what you'd like, and no doubt it'll please him. What do you say to that cruet-stand?"

"Damn the cruet-stand!" said Trimblett, wiping his hot face.

"All right," said the unmoved Walsh, with his arm firmly linked in that of his friend. "What about a toast-rack? That one!"

"I don't believe in wedding-presents," said Trimblett, thickly. "Never did. I think it's an absurd custom. And if your friend says he isn't going to be married, surely he ought to know."

"Shyness," rejoined Captain Walsh—"pure shyness. He's one of the best. I know his idea. His idea is to be married on the quiet and without any fuss. But it isn't coming off. No, sir. Now, suppose it was you—don't be violent; I only said suppose—how would that pickle-jar strike you?"

"I know nothing about it," said Captain Trimblett, raising his voice. "Besides, I can't take the responsibility of choosing for another man. I told you so before."

Captain Walsh paid no heed. His glance roved over the contents of the window.

"Trimblett's a terror," he said in a serene voice, turning to Hartley. "I don't know what it's like walking down the High Street looking into shop-windows with a fretful porcupine; but I can make a pretty good guess."

"You should leave me alone, then," said Trimblett, wrenching his arm free. "Wedding-presents have no interest for me."

"That's what he keeps saying," said Walsh, turning to Hartley again; "and when I referred just now—in the most delicate manner—to love's young dream, I thought he'd ha' bust his boilers."

As far as Hartley could see, Captain Trimblett was again within measurable distance of such a catastrophe. For a moment he struggled wildly for speech, and then, coming to the conclusion that nothing he could say would do him any good, he swung on his heel and walked off. Hartley, with a nod to Walsh, followed.

"That idiot has been pestering me for the last half-hour," said Captain Trimblett, after walking for some distance in wrathful silence. "I wonder whether it would be brought in murder if I wrung old Sellers's neck? I've had four people this morning come up and talk to me about getting married. At least, they started talking."

"Turn a deaf ear," said Hartley.

"Deaf ear?" repeated the captain. "I wish I could. The last few days I've been wishing that I hadn't got ears. It's all Truefitt's doing. He's hinting now that I'm too bashful to speak up, and that weak-headed Cecilia Willett believes him. If you could only see her fussing round and trying to make things easy for me, as she considers, you'd wonder I don't go crazy."

"We've all got our troubles," said Hartley, shaking his head.

The indignant-captain turned and regarded him fiercely.

"I am likely to leave Vyner and Son," said the other, slowly, "after thirty-five years."

The wrath died out of the captain's face, and he regarded his old friend with looks of affectionate concern. In grim silence he listened to an account of the interview with Mr. Vyner.

"You know what it all means," he said, savagely, as Hartley finished.

"I—I think so," was the reply.

"It means," said the captain, biting his words—"it means that unless Joan is married within three months, so as to be out of Robert Vyner's way, you will be dismissed the firm. It saves the old man's pride a bit putting it that way, and it's safer, too. And if Robert Vyner marries her he will have to earn his own living. With luck he might get thirty shillings a week."

"I know," said the other.

"Get her to town as soon as possible," continued the captain, impressively. He paused a moment, and added with some feeling, "That's what I'm going to do; I spoke to Mr. Vyner about it to-day. We will go up together, and I'll look after her."

"I'll write to-night," said Hartley. "Not that it will make any difference, so far as I can see."

"It's a step in the right direction, at any rate," retorted the captain. "It keeps her out of young Vyner's way, and it shows John Vyner that you are doing your best to meet his views, and it might make him realize that you have got a little pride, too."

Partly to cheer Hartley up, and partly to avoid returning to Tranquil Vale, he spent the evening with him, and, being deterred by the presence of Miss Hartley from expressing his opinion of John Vyner, indulged instead in a violent tirade against the tyranny of wealth. Lured on by the highly interested Joan, he went still further, and in impassioned words committed himself to the statement that all men were equal, and should have equal rights, only hesitating when he discovered that she had been an unwilling listener on an occasion when he had pointed out to an offending seaman certain blemishes in his family tree. He then changed the subject to the baneful practice of eavesdropping.

By the time he reached home it was quite late. There was no moon, but the heavens were bright with stars. He stood outside for a few moments listening to the sound of voices within, and then, moved perhaps by the quiet beauty of the night, strolled down to the river and stood watching the lights of passing craft. Midnight sounded in the distance as he walked back.

The lamp was still burning, but the room was empty. He closed the door softly behind him, and stood eying, with some uneasiness, a large and untidy brown-paper parcel that stood in the centre of the table. From the crumpled appearance of the paper and the clumsily tied knots it had the appearance of having been opened and fastened up again by unskilled hands. The sense of uneasiness deepened as he approached the table and stood, with his head on one side, looking at it.

He turned at the sound of a light shuffling step in the kitchen. The door opened gently and the head of Mr. Truefitt was slowly inserted. Glimpses of a shirt and trousers, and the rumpled condition of the intruder's hair, suggested that he had newly risen from bed.

"I heard you come in," he said, in a stealthy whisper.

"Yes?" said the captain.

"There was no address on it," said Mr. Truefitt, indicating the parcel by a nod; "it was left by somebody while we were out, and on opening it we found it was for you. At least, partly. I thought I ought to tell you."

"It don't matter," said the captain, with an effort.

Mr. Truefitt nodded again. "I only wanted to explain how it was," he said. "Good-night."

He closed the door behind him, and the captain, after eying the parcel for some time, drew a clasp-knife from his pocket and with trembling fingers cut the string and stripped off the paper. The glistening metal of the largest electro-plated salad-bowl he had ever seen met his horrified gaze. In a hypnotized fashion he took out the fork and spoon and balanced them in his fingers. A small card at the bottom of the bowl caught his eye, and he bent over and read it:—

"With Hearty Congratulations and Best Wishes to Captain and Mrs. Trimblett from Captain Michael Walsh."

For a long time he stood motionless; then, crumpling the card up and placing it in his pocket, he took the bowl in his arms and bore it to his bedroom. Wrapped again in its coverings, it was left to languish on the top of the cupboard behind a carefully constructed rampart of old cardboard boxes and worn-out books.

CHAPTER XIV

Mr. Hartley's idea, warmly approved by Captain Trimblett, was to divulge the state of affairs to his daughter in much the same circuitous fashion that Mr. Vyner had revealed it to him. He had not taken into account, however, the difference in temper of the listeners, and one or two leading questions from Joan brought the matter to an abrupt conclusion. She sat divided between wrath and dismay.

"You—you must have misunderstood him," she said at last, with a little gasp. "He could not be so mean, and tyrannical, and ridiculous."

Her father shook his head. "There is no room for misunderstanding," he said, quietly. "Still, I have got three months to look about me, and I don't suppose we shall starve."

Miss Hartley expressed the wish—as old as woman—to give the offender a piece of her mind. She also indulged in a few general remarks concerning the obtuseness of people who were unable to see when they were not wanted, by which her father understood her to refer to Vyner junior.

"I was afraid you cared for him," he said, awkwardly.

"I?" exclaimed Joan, in the voice of one unable to believe her ears. "Oh, father, I am surprised at you; I never thought you would say such a thing."

Mr. Hartley eyed her uneasily.

"Why should you think anything so absurd?" continued his daughter, with some severity.

Mr. Hartley, with much concern, began to cite a long list of things responsible for what he freely admitted was an unfortunate mistake on his part. His daughter listened with growing impatience and confusion, and, as he showed no signs of nearing the end, rose in a dignified fashion and quitted the room. She was back, however, in a minute or two, and, putting her arm on his shoulder, bent down and kissed him.

"I had no idea you were so observant," she remarked, softly.

"I don't think I am really," said the conscientious man. "If it hadn't been for Trimblett—"

Miss Hartley, interrupting with spirit, paid a tribute to the captain that ought to have made his ears burn.

"I ought to have been more careful all these years," said her father presently. "If I had, this would not have mattered so much. Prodigality never pays—"

Joan placed her arm about his neck again. "Prodigality!" she said, with a choking laugh. "You don't know the meaning of the word. And you have had to help other people all your life. After all, perhaps you and Captain Trimblett are wrong; Mr. Vyner can't be in earnest, it is too absurd."

"Yes, he is," said Hartley, sitting up, with a sudden air of determination. "But then, so am I. I am not going to be dictated to in this fashion. My private affairs are nothing to do with him. I—I shall have to tell him so."

"Don't do anything yet," said Joan, softly, as she resumed her seat. "By the way—"

"Well?" said her father, after a pause.

"That invitation from Uncle William was your doing," continued Joan, levelling an incriminating finger at him.

"Trimblett's idea," said her father, anxious to give credit where it was due. "His idea was that if you were to go away for a time Robert Vyner would very likely forget all about you."

"I'm not afraid of that," said Joan, with a slight smile. "I mean—I mean—what business has Captain Trimblett to concern himself about my affairs?"

"I know what you mean," said Hartley, in a low voice.

He got up, and crossing to the window stood looking out on his beloved garden. His thoughts went back to the time, over twenty years ago, when he and his young wife had planted it. He remembered that in those far-off days she had looked forward with confidence to the time when he would be offered a share in the firm. For a moment he felt almost glad—

"I suppose that Captain Trimblett is right," said Joan, who had been watching him closely; "and I'll go when you like."

Her father came from the window. "Yes," he said, and stood looking at her.

"I am going out a little way," said Joan, suddenly.

Hartley started, and glanced instinctively at the clock. "Yes," he said again.

His daughter went upstairs to dress, and did her best to work up a little resentment against being turned out of her home to avoid a caller whom she told herself repeatedly she had no wish to see. Her reflections were cut short by remembering that time was passing, and that Mr. Vyner's punctuality, in the matter of these calls, was of a nature to which the office was a stranger.

She put on her hat and, running downstairs, opened the door and went out. At the gate she paused, and, glancing right and left, saw Robert Vyner approaching. He bowed and quickened his pace.

"Father is indoors," she said with a friendly smile, as she shook hands.

"It's a sin to be indoors an evening like this," said Robert, readily. "Are you going for a walk?"

"A little way; I am going to see a friend," said Joan. "Good-by."

"Good-by," said Mr. Vyner, and turned in at the gate, while Joan, a little surprised at his docility, proceeded on her way. She walked slowly, trying, in the interests of truth, to think of some acquaintance to call upon. Then she heard footsteps behind, gradually gaining upon her.

"I really think I'm the most forgetful man in Salt-haven," said Mr. Robert Vyner, in tones of grave annoyance, as he ranged alongside. "I came all this way to show your father a book on dahlias, and now I find I've left it at the office. What's a good thing for a bad memory?"

"Punish yourself by running all the way, I should think," replied Joan. "It might make you less forgetful next time."

Mr. Vyner became thoughtful, not to say grave. "I don't know so much about running," he said, slowly. "I've had an idea for some time past that my heart is a little bit affected."

Joan turned to him swiftly. "I'm so sorry," she faltered. "I had no idea; and the other night you were rolling the grass. Why didn't you speak of it before?"

Her anxiety was so genuine that Mr. Vyner had the grace to feel a little bit ashamed of himself.

"When I say that my heart is affected, I don't mean in the way of—of disease," he murmured.

"Is it weak?" inquired the girl.

Mr. Vyner shook his head.

"Well, what is the matter with it?"

Mr. Vyner sighed. "I don't know," he said, slowly. "It is not of long standing; I only noticed it a little while ago. The first time I had an attack I was sitting in my office—working. Let me see. I think it was the day you came in there to see your father. Yes, I am sure it was."

Miss Hartley walked on, looking straight before her.

"Since then," pursued Mr. Vyner, in the mournful tones suited to the subject, "it has got gradually worse. Sometimes it is in my mouth; sometimes—if I feel that I have offended anybody—it is in my boots."

Miss Hartley paid no heed.

"It is in my boots now," said the invalid, plaintively; "tight boots, too. Do you know what I was thinking just now when you looked at me in that alarmed, compassionate way?"

"Not alarmed," muttered Miss Hartley.

"I was thinking," pursued Mr. Vyner, in a rapt voice, "I was thinking what a fine nurse you would make. Talking of heart troubles put it in my mind, I suppose. Fancy being down for a month or two with a complaint that didn't hurt or take one's appetite away, and having you for a nurse!"

"I think that if you are going to talk nonsense—" began Joan, half stopping.

"I'm not," said the other, in alarm, "I've quite finished; I have, indeed."

He stole a glance at the prim young, figure by his side, and his voice again developed a plaintive note. "If you only knew what it was like," he continued, "to be mewed up in an office all day, with not a soul to speak to, and the sun shining, perhaps you'd make allowances."

"I saw you down by the harbour this morning," said the girl.

"Harbour?" said the other, pretending to reflect—"this morning?"

Joan nodded. "Yes; you were lounging about—in the sunshine—smoking a cigarette. Then you went on to the Indian Chief and stood talking for, oh, quite a long time to Captain Trimblett. Then—"

"Yes?" breathed Mr. Vyner, as she paused in sudden confusion. "What did I do next?"

Miss Hartley shook her head. "I only saw you for a moment," she said.

Mr. Vyner did not press the matter; he talked instead on other subjects, but there was a tenderness in his voice for which Miss Hartley told herself her own thoughtlessness was largely responsible. She trembled and walked a little faster. Then, with a sense of relief, she saw Captain Trimblett approaching them. His head was bent in thought, and his usual smile was missing as he looked up and saw them.

"I wanted to see you," he said to Joan. "I'm off to London to-morrow."

"To-morrow!" repeated the girl, in surprise.

"Twelve-thirty train," said the captain, looking shrewdly from one to the other. "I'm just off home; there are one or two matters I must attend to before I go, and I wanted to talk to you."

"I will come with you," said Joan, quickly. "I haven't seen Mrs. Chinnery for a long time." She nodded to Mr. Vyner and held out her hand. "Good-by."

"Good-by," said that gentleman. He shook hands reluctantly, and his amiable features took on a new expression as he glanced at the captain.

"Try and cheer him up," he said, with an air of false concern. "It's only for a little while, cap'n; you'll soon be back and—you know the old adage?"

"Yes," said the captain, guardedly.

"Although, of course, there are several," said Mr. Vyner, thoughtfully. "I wonder whether we were thinking of the same one?"

"I dare say," said the other, hastily.

"I was thinking of 'Absence makes the heart grow fonder'—of the Indian Chief" said the ingenuous Robert. "Was that the one you were thinking of?"

The captain's reply was inaudible as he turned and bore off Miss Hartley. The young man stood for some time watching them, and, as Joan and her burly companion disappeared round the corner, shook his head and set off home.

"He'll sober down as he gets older," said the captain, after they had proceeded some way in silence. "I'm glad I met you. Your father told me you were going to London, and I was thinking we might go up together. It's odd we should both be going. Quite a coincidence."

"In more ways than one," said Joan. "Father told me you had arranged it together. I quite know why I am going."

The captain coughed.

"I know why you are going, too," said Joan.

The captain coughed again, and muttered something about "children" and "business."

"And if I'm going to-morrow I had better get back and pack," continued the girl.

"Plenty of time in the morning," said the captain. "It'll make the time pass. It's a mistake to stow your things away too soon—a great mistake."

"I would sooner do it, though," said Joan, pausing. 170

"You come along to Tranquil Vale," said Captain Trimblett, with forced joviality. "Never mind about your packing. Stay to supper, and I'll see you home afterward."

Miss Hartley eyed him thoughtfully.

"Why?" she inquired.

"Pleasure of your company," said the captain.

"Why?" said Miss Hartley again.

The captain eyed her thoughtfully in his turn.

"I—I haven't told 'em I'm going yet," he said, slowly. "It'll be a little surprise to them, perhaps. Miss Willett will be there. She's a silly thing. She and Peter might make a duet about it If you are there—"

"I'll take care of you," said Joan, with a benevolent smile. "You'll be safe with me. What a pity you didn't bring your little troubles to me at first!"

The captain turned a lurid eye upon her, and then, realizing that silence was more dignified and certainly safer than speech, said nothing. He walked on with head erect and turned a deaf ear to the faint sounds which Miss Hartley was endeavouring to convert into coughs.

Mrs. Chinnery, who was sitting alone in the front room, rose and greeted her with some warmth as she entered, and, the usual reproachful question put and answered as to the length of time since her last visit, took her hat from her and went upstairs with it. An arch smile from Miss Hartley during her absence was met by the ungrateful captain with a stony stare.

"I came to bid you good-by," said Joan, as Mrs. Chinnery returned. "I am off to London to-morrow."

"London!" said Mrs. Chinnery.

"I am going to stay with an uncle," replied Joan.

"Quite a coincidence, isn't it?" said the captain, averting his gaze from the smiling face of Miss Hartley, and trying to keep his voice level.

"Coincidence!" said Mrs. Chinnery, staring at him.

"I've got to go, too," said the captain, with what he fondly imagined was a casual smile. "Got to run up and see my boys and girls. Just a flying visit there and back. So we are going together."

"You!" said the astonished Mrs. Chinnery. "Why didn't you tell me? Why, I've got nothing ready. Serves me right for putting things off."

The captain began to murmur something about an urgent letter, but Mrs. Chinnery, who had opened the cupboard and brought out a work-basket containing several pairs of the thick woollen socks that formed the captain's usual wear, was almost too busy to listen. She threaded a needle, and, drawing a sock over her left hand, set to work on a gaping wound that most women would have regarded as mortal.

Mr. Truefitt and Mrs. Willett entered from the garden just as the Captain was explaining for the third time.

"Children are not ill, I hope," said Mr. Truefitt with ill concealed anxiety.

"No," said the Captain.

Mrs. Willett had seated herself by the side of Mrs. Chinnery, ventured to pat that lady's busy hand.

"He will soon be back," she murmured.

"He will look after that," said Mr. Truefitt, with a boisterous laugh. "Won't you, cap'n?"

Miss Willett sat regarding Captain Trimblett with a pensive air. She was beginning to regard his diffidence and shyness as something abnormal. Hints of the most helpful nature only seemed to add to his discomfort, and she began to doubt whether he would ever muster up sufficient resolution to put an end to a situation that was fast becoming embarrassing to all concerned.

"Of course," she said, suddenly, "it is only right that you should run up and see your children first. I hadn't thought of that."

"First?" repeated the captain, his face flooding with colour as he realized the inward meaning of the remark. "What do you mean by first?"

His voice was so loud that Miss Willett sat up with a start and looked round nervously.

"Miss Willett means before you sail," said Joan, gently, before that lady could speak. "How pleased they will be to see you!"

"Aye, aye," said the captain, regaining his composure by an effort.

"What a lot of things he will have to tell them!" murmured the persevering Miss Willett. "Have you ever seen them?" she inquired, turning to Mrs. Chinnery.

"No," was the reply.

"How strange!" said Miss Willett, with a reproachful glance at the captain. "I expect you'll like them very much when you do."

"Sure to," chimed in Mr. Truefitt. "Susanna was always partial to children."

"I'm sure she is," said Miss Willett, regarding the industrious Mrs. Chinnery affectionately. "How fortunate!"

She rose as she spoke, and, screwing her face up at Joan with great significance, asked her whether she wouldn't care to see the garden.

"Very much," said Joan. "Come along," she added, turning to the captain. "Now come and show me that rose-bush you have been talking about so much."

Captain Trimblett rose with an alacrity that mystified Miss Willett more than ever, and, having gained the garden, found so many things to show Miss Hartley, and so much to talk about, that supper was on the table before he had finished. Fearful of being left alone with Miss Willett, he stuck to his young protector so closely that in going in at the door he trod on her heel. Miss Hartley entered the room limping, and, having gained her seat, sat eying him with an expression in which pain and reproachful mirth struggled for the mastery.

"What a delightful evening!" she said, in an affected voice, as the captain walked home with her about an hour later; "I have enjoyed myself tremendously."

The captain uttered an impatient exclamation.

"It reminded me of the old fable of the lion and the mouse," continued Joan.

The captain grunted again, and, in a voice that he vainly endeavoured to render polite, said that he did not know what she was talking about.

CHAPTER XV

Mr. Robert Vyner received the news of Miss Hartley's sudden departure with an air of polite interest. The secrecy of the affair and the fact that she had gone with Captain Trimblett convinced him that it was no casual visit, and he mused bitterly on the strange tendency of seafaring people to meddle with the affairs of others. An attempt to ascertain from Hartley the probable duration of her visit, and other interesting particulars, as they sat together in the young man's office, yielded no satisfaction.

"She made up her mind to go rather suddenly, didn't she?" he inquired.

Hartley said "Yes," and murmured something about taking advantage of the opportunity of going up with Captain Trimblett. "She is very fond of the captain," he added.

"Is she staying near him?" asked Vyner, without looking up from his work.

The chief clerk, who was anxious to get away, said "No," and eyed him uneasily.

"I hope that London will agree with her," continued Robert, politely. "Is she staying in a healthy part?"

"Very," said the other.

Mr. Vyner bent over his work again, and scowled diabolically at an innocent letter which said that his instructions should have immediate attention. "Which do you consider a healthy part?" he said presently.

Mr. Hartley, after some reflection, said there were many districts which merited that description. He mentioned eleven, and was discoursing somewhat learnedly on drainage and soils when he noticed that the young man's attention was wandering. With a muttered reference to his work, he rose and quitted the room.

Day succeeded day in tiresome waiting, and Mr. Robert Vyner, leaning back in his chair, regarded with a hostile eye the pile of work that accumulated on his table as he sat dreaming of Joan Hartley. In a species of waking nightmare he would see her beset by hordes of respectful but persistent admirers. He manifested a craving for Mr. Hartley's society, and, discovering by actual experience that, melancholy as the house was without its mistress, all other places were more melancholy still, contrived, to its owner's great discomfort, to spend a considerable number of his evenings there.

"He's a pattern to all of you," said Rosa to Mr. Walters, who sat in the kitchen one evening, cautiously watching Mr. Vyner through a small hole in the muslin blind.

Mr. Walters grunted.

"I believe he worships the ground she treads on," said Rosa, in exalted tones.

Mr. Walters grunted again, and her colour rose. For nearly a fortnight she had not spoken to any other man—at least, to the boatswain's knowledge—and she fully realized the cloying effect of security upon a man of his temperament.

"Last night I saw him standing for half an hour looking into a shop," she said, softly. "What shop do you think it was?"

Mr. Walters's face took on an obstinate expression. "Butcher's?" he hazarded, at last.

"Butcher's!" repeated Rosa, with scorn. "What should he want to look in a butcher's for? It was Hickman's, the jeweller's."

The boatswain said "Oh!" and devoted himself with renewed interest to his task of watching Mr. Vyner. Miss Jelks's conversation for some time past had circled round engagement-rings, a subject which brought him face to face with the disagreeable side of flirtation.

"More fool him," he said, without looking round.

Rosa gazed fixedly at the back of his head. She was far too sensible not to have noticed the gradual waning of his passion, and she chided herself severely for having dropped her usual tactics. At the same time she realized that she was not alone to blame in the matter, the gilded youth of Salthaven, after one or two encounters with Mr. Walters, having come to the conclusion that a flirtation with her was a temptation to be avoided.

"Most men are fools," she said, calmly. "A young fellow I met the other evening—the night you couldn't come out—went on like a madman just because I wouldn't promise to meet him again."

"Pity I didn't see 'im," said Mr. Walters, grimly.

"Oh!" said Rosa, losing her head. "Why?"

"I'd ha' give 'im something to make a fuss about," said the boatswain, "that's all."

"It's not his fault," said Rosa, softly. "He couldn't help himself. He told me so. Quite the gentleman— quite. You ought to see the way he raises his hat. And his head is covered all over with little short curls."

"Like a nigger," said Mr. Walters, with disappointing calmness.

He removed his eye from the window and, taking out his pipe, began to fill it from a small metal box. Rosa, compressing her lips, watched him with a sardonic smile.

"Got anything to do this evening?" she inquired.

"No," said the other.

"Well, I have," said Rosa, with a bright smile, "so I'll say good-evening."

Mr. Walters rose and, replacing a box of matches in his pocket, stood watching her with his mouth open.

"Don't hurry," she said, at last.

The boatswain sat down again.

"I mean when you get outside," explained the girl.

Mr. Walters gazed at her in slow perplexity, and then, breathing heavily, walked out of the kitchen like a man in a dream. His suspicions were aroused, and with an idea that a little blood-letting would give him relief, he wasted the entire evening lying in wait for a good-looking, gentlemanly young man with curly hair.

Miss Jelks waited for his appearance the following evening in vain. Several evenings passed, but no boatswain, and it became apparent at last that he had realized the perils of his position. Anger at his defection was mingled with admiration for his strength of mind every time she looked in the glass.

She forged her weapons slowly. A new hat was ready, but a skirt and coat still languished at the dressmaker's. She waited until they came home, and then, dressing her hair in a style which owed something to a fashion-paper and something to her lack of skill, sallied out to put matters on a more satisfactory footing.

It was early evening, and the street fairly full, but for some time she wandered about aimlessly. Twice she smiled at young men of her acquaintance, and they smiled back and went on their way. The third she met with a smile so inviting that against his better sense he stopped, and after a nervous glance round made a remark about the weather.

"Beautiful," said Rosa. "Have you been ill, Mr. Filer?"

"Ill?" said the young man, staring. "No. Why?"

"Haven't seen you for such a long time," said Miss Jelks, swinging her parasol. "I've been wondering what had become of you. I was afraid you were ill."

Mr. Filer caressed his moustache. "I haven't seen you about," he retorted.

"I haven't been out lately," said the girl; "it's so lonely walking about by yourself that I'd sooner sit indoors and mope."

Mr. Filer stood blinking thoughtfully. "I s'pose you're going to meet a friend?" he said, at last.

"No," said Rosa. "I s'pose you are?"

Mr. Filer said "No" in his turn.

Two minutes later, in a state of mind pretty evenly divided between trepidation and joy, he found himself walking by her side.

They chose at first the quietest streets, but under Miss Jelks's guidance drifted slowly back to the town.

To her annoyance the boatswain was nowhere to be seen, and the idea of wasting the evening in the society of Mr. Filer annoyed her beyond measure. She became moody, and vague in her replies to his sallies, seated herself on a pile of timber, and motioned the young man to join her and finally, with the forlorn hope that Mr. Walters might be spending the evening aboard ship, strolled on to the quay.

Work was over and they had the place to themselves.

She seated herself on a pile of timber and, motioning the young man to join her, experienced a sudden thrill as she saw the head of Mr. Walters protruding tortoise-like over the side of the Indian Chief, which lay a little way below them. Fearful that Mr. Filer should see it, she directed his attention to two small boys who were disporting themselves in a ship's boat, and, with her head almost on his shoulder, blotted out the steamer with three feathers and a bunch of roses.

It was a beautiful evening, but Mr. Filer failed to understand why she should slap his hand when he said so. He could hardly open his mouth without being requested to behave himself and getting another tiny slap. Greatly encouraged by this treatment he ventured to pass his left arm round her waist, and, in full view of the choking boatswain, imprison both her hands in his.

Miss Jelks endured it for two minutes, and then, breaking away, gave him a playful little prod with her parasol and fled behind a warehouse uttering faint shrieks. Mr. Filer gave chase at once, in happy ignorance that his rival had nearly fallen overboard in a hopeless attempt to see round the corner. Flesh and blood could stand it no longer, and when the couple emerged and began to walk in a more sober fashion toward the town an infuriated boatswain followed a little in the rear.

Mr. Filer saw him first and, with a sudden sinking at his heart, dropped his light banter and began to discourse on more serious subjects. He attempted to widen the distance between them, but in vain. A second glance showed him Mr. Walters close behind, with a face like that of two destroying angels rolled into one. Trembling with fright he quickened his pace and looked round eagerly for means of escape. His glance fell on a confectioner's window, and muttering the word "Ice" he dashed in, followed in a more leisurely fashion by Miss Jelks.

"I was just feeling like an ice," she said, as she took a seat at a little marble-topped table. She put her hat straight in a mirror opposite, and removing her gloves prepared for action.

Mr. Filer ate his ice mechanically, quite unaware of its flavour; then as nothing happened he plucked up courage and began to talk. His voice shook a little at first, but was gradually getting stronger, when he broke off suddenly with his spoon in mid-air and gazed in fascinated horror at a disc of greenish-yellow nose that pressed against the shop-window. The eyes behind it looked as though they might melt the glass.

He put his spoon down on the table and tried to think. Miss Jelks finished her ice and sat smiling at him.

"Could you—could you eat another?" he faltered.

Miss Jelks said that she could try, and remarked, casually, that she had once eaten thirteen, and had shared the usual superstition concerning that number ever since.

"Aren't you going to have one, too?" she inquired, when the fresh ice arrived.

Mr. Filer shook his head, and, trying hard to ignore the face at the window, said that he was not hungry. He sat trembling with agitation, and, desirous of postponing the encounter with the boatswain as long as possible, kept ordering ices for Miss Jelks until that lady, in justice to herself, declined to eat any more.

"I can't finish this," she said. "You'll have to help me."

She took up a generous spoonful, and in full view of the face at the window leaned across the table and put it into Mr. Filer's unwilling mouth. With a violent shudder he saw the boatswain leave the window and take up a position in front of the door. Miss Jelks drew on her gloves and, with another glance in the mirror as she rose, turned to leave. Mr. Filer made no attempt to follow.

"Ain't you ready?" said Miss Jelks, pausing.

"I'm not feeling very well," said the young man, desperately, as he passed his hand across his forehead. "It's the ice, I think—I'm not used to 'em."

"Perhaps the air will do you good," said Rosa.

Mr. Filer shook his head. Whatever good the air might do him would, he felt certain, be counteracted by the treatment of the boatswain.

"Don't wait for me," he said, with a faint sad smile. "I might be here for hours; I've been like it before."

"I can't leave you like this," said Rosa. "Why"—she turned suddenly, and her face lit up with a smile—"here's Mr. Walters! How fortunate! He'll be able to help you home."

"No—don't trouble," gasped Mr. Filer, as the boatswain came into the shop and prepared to render first aid by moistening his palms and rubbing them together. "It's very kind of you, but I shall be all right if I'm left alone. I'd rather be left alone—I would indeed."

"You'd better let the gentleman help you home," urged the shopkeeper. "He looks strong."

Mr. Filer shuddered.

"And you can lean on me," said Rosa, softly.

Mr. Filer shuddered again, and with surprising energy, considering his invalid condition, gripped the iron frame of the table with his legs and clutched the top with his hands.

"I don't like leaving him here," said Rosa, hesitating.

"Neither don't I," growled the boatswain. "'Ow-ever, I s'pose I'll run against 'im sooner or later."

He escorted Rosa to the door and, after a yearning glance at Mr. Filer, followed her out and walked by her side in silence.

"Poor fellow," said Rosa, at last. "How generous he is! I believe he'd give me anything I asked for."

Mr. Walters started and, bending his brows, muttered something about giving Mr. Filer more than he asked for.

"Oh, yes; I dare say," retorted Rosa, turning on him with sudden heat. "I'm not to speak to anybody to please you. You leave my friends alone. What's it got to do with you?"

"I see you," said Mr. Walters, darkly; "I see you from the ship. You little thought as 'ow I was a watching your little games."

Miss Jelks stopped and, drawing herself up, regarded him haughtily.

"I didn't ask you for your company, Mr. Walters," she said, sharply, "so you can take yourself off as soon as you like."

She turned and walked off in the opposite direction, and Mr. Walters, after a moment's hesitation, turned and followed. They walked in this fashion for some distance; then the boatswain, quickening his pace, caught her roughly by the arm.

"I want to show you something," he growled.

Miss Jelks eyed him disdainfully.

"In 'ere," said the other, pointing to the same jeweller's window that had been the cause of so much discomfort to Captain Trimblett.

"Well?" said the girl, her eyes sparkling.

For answer the gentle swain took her by the elbows and propelled her into the shop, and approaching the counter gazed disagreeably at the shopman.

"I want a ring for this young lady," he said, reddening despite himself. "A good 'un—one o' the best."

The man turned to the window and, after a little careful groping, unhooked a velvet card studded with rings. Rosa's eyes shone, but she drew off her glove with a fine show of unwillingness at the boatswain's command.

"Try that on," he said, pointing to a ring.

Miss Jelks placed it on the third finger of her left hand, and holding it up to the light gazed at it entranced.

"'Ow much?" said the boatswain, jerking his head.

"That's a very nice ring," said the assistant.

"Twenty—" he referred to a tiny label on the card, "twenty-five pounds."

The boatswain's jaw dropped, and both listeners made noble efforts to appear unconscious that his breathing was anything out of the ordinary.

"Take it off," he said, as soon as he could speak; "take it off at once."

"It's too large," said Rosa, with a sigh.

She drew it off, and, turning to a case the jeweller placed before her, tried on several more. Suited at last, she held up her hand with the ring on it for Mr. Walters's inspection.

"It fits beautifully," she said, softly, as the boatswain scratched the back of his neck.

"A very nice ring, that," said the assistant. "A queen might wear it."

"Take it off," cried Mr. Walters, hastily.

"Seventeen shillings and sixpence," said the jeweller, almost as quickly.

"I like it better than the other," said Rosa.

"It is better," said the boatswain, in a relieved voice.

He counted out the money and, turning a deaf but blushing ear to the jeweller's glowing description of his wedding-rings, led the way outside. Rosa took his arm and leaned on it heavily.

"Fancy! We are engaged now," she said, squeezing his arm and looking up at him.

Mr. Walters, who seemed to be in a state of considerable perturbation, made no reply.

"Fancy you being in such a hurry!" continued Rosa, with another squeeze.

"It's a failing of mine," said the boatswain, still staring straight before him. "Always was."

CHAPTER XVI

Joan Hartley's ideas of London, gathered from books and illustrated papers, were those of a town to which her uncle and aunt were utter strangers. Mr. William Carr knew Cornhill and the adjacent district thoroughly, and thirty or forty years before had made periodical descents upon the West-end. He left home at half-past eight every morning and returned every evening at five minutes to six, except on Saturdays, when he returned at ten minutes past three, and spent his half holiday in the dining-room reading an early edition of the evening paper. Any paragraphs relating to Royalty were read aloud to his wife, who knew not only all the members of the English Royal Family by name, but also those dignitaries abroad who had the happiness to be connected with it in marriage. She could in all probability have given the King himself much useful information as to the ages and fourth and fifth Christian names of some of the later and more remote members of his family.

Her day was as regular and methodical as her husband's. The morning was devoted to assisting and superintending the general servant for the time being; after dinner, at one o'clock, she retired upstairs to dress and went down to the shops to make a few purchases, returning in good time to give her husband tea. The early part of the evening was devoted to waiting for supper; the latter part to waiting for bed.

During the first week of Joan's visit an agreeable thrill was communicated to the household by preparations for an evening, or perhaps an afternoon and evening, in town. The event came off—in the third week of her stay—on a wet Thursday afternoon, Mrs. Carr and Joan got wet walking to the omnibus, and wetter still waiting at one corner of the Bank of England for Mr. Carr, who was getting wet at another.

Mr. Carr, who was in holiday attire, was smoking a large cigar in honour of the occasion, which he extinguished upon entering an omnibus and re-lighted at the Zoological Gardens. By the aid of careful manipulation and the rain it lasted him until evening. They wound up an eventful day at a theatre, and Mr. Carr, being anxious to do the thing well, took them all the way home in a four-wheeler. A little sum in mental arithmetic, which he worked on the way and submitted to the cabman at the end of the journey, was found to be wrong.

The outing was not repeated. Mrs. Carr went about for a day or two with the air of one who had returned from a long and fatiguing expedition; and her husband, when he returned from business the day following and changed into his slippers, paid such a warm tribute to the joys and comforts of home that his niece abandoned all ideas of any further jaunts. Wearied by the dulness and the monotony of the streets, she began to count the days till her return. Her father's letters made no mention of it; but the Salthaven news in them only increased her eagerness.

She returned one day from a solitary ramble on Hampstead Heath to find that Salthaven, or a whiff of it, had come to her. A deep voice, too well known to be mistaken, fell on her ears as she entered the front door, and hastening to the drawing-room she found her aunt entertaining Captain Trimblett to afternoon tea. One large hand balanced a cup and saucer; the other held a plate. His method of putting both articles in one hand while he ate or drank might have excited the envy of a practised juggler. When Joan entered the room she found her aunt, with her eyes riveted on a piece of the captain's buttered toast that was lying face downward on the carpet, carrying on a disjointed conversation.

"I just looked in," said the captain, as Joan almost embraced him. "Mind the tea!"

"Looked in?" echoed Joan.

"One tram, three buses—one of 'em a mistake—and my own legs," said the captain. "I had no idea it was so far."

"People have no idea how far out we really are," said Mrs. Carr, looking round with a satisfied smile. "I've noticed it before. Did you find the air different, Captain Trimblett?"

"Very," said the captain with a sudden gasp, as he caught sight of the piece of toast. "Very fine air. Very fine. Very—quite strong."

He shifted his feet restlessly and the toast disappeared. For a moment Mrs. Carr thought that the floor had opened and swallowed it up. Realizing that the day of useful miracles had passed, she gazed fixedly at his left foot.

"Well," said the captain, turning a relieved face to Joan, "how is the round of gayety? Are you tired of being a butterfly yet? I suppose after this Salt-haven won't be good enough for you?"

"There's nothing like life for young people," said Mrs. Carr. "Give them plenty of life and that's all they want."

Miss Hartley, whose back was toward her aunt, made a grimace.

"It's very natural," said the captain.

Miss Hartley made a further effort—one that she had relinquished at the age of ten—but the captain, intent upon a bite, missed it.

"In my young days all I thought of was gadding about," said Mrs. Carr, smiling. "I wasn't very strong either; it was just my spirits kept me up. But I used to suffer for it afterward."

"We all do," said the captain, politely.

By a feat of absolute legerdemain he took out his handkerchief and brushed some crumbs from his beard. His cup slid to the edge of the saucer and peeped over, but, throwing the spoon overboard, righted itself just in time. Somewhat pleased with himself he replaced the handkerchief and, drinking the remainder of his tea, thankfully handed the crockery to Joan. After which, with a mind relieved, he-sat and spun his marvelling hostess a few tales of the sea.

He left under plea of business, before Mr. Carr's return, and with a reference to the family likeness obtaining between omnibuses, asked Joan to see him safe aboard. He accompanied the request with such a distortion of visage that she rightly concluded that he wished for an opportunity to speak to her alone.

"You're looking better," he said, when they got outside. "A year or two in London will be the making of you."

"A year or two!" echoed the startled Joan. "I've had quite enough of it already, thank you. I've never been so dull."

"You haven't got used to the change yet," said the captain, indulgently. "That's natural; but in another month I expect you'll have quite a different tale to tell."

"I am going home next weak," said Miss Hartley, in a decided voice.

Captain Trimblett coughed.

"Why shouldn't I?" inquired the girl, in reply.

The captain coughed again.

"I should think the Carrs would be glad to have you," he replied, becoming suddenly busy with his handkerchief, "especially as they have got no children. And a year or two with them in town would give you a—a sort of finish."

"You have heard something from my father?" exclaimed Joan, turning on him.

"He—he wrote," said the captain.

"Did he suggest my staying here?"

"No," said the captain, putting his handkerchief away with great care. "No, I can't say he did. But he has had another interview with Mr. John Vyner, and it seems that the old gentleman is quite taking it for granted that you have left Salthaven for good. He was quite genial to your father."

"Did father undeceive him?" inquired the girl.

"He didn't say," rejoined the other. "My idea is he didn't; but it's only my idea, mind."

For some time Miss Hartley walked on in disdainful silence. She broke it at last in favour of Mr. Vyner, senior.

"Talking won't alter facts, though," said the admiring captain, shaking his head.

The girl paid no heed.

"Now, if you only stayed here for a little while," said the captain, persuasively, "say a couple of years, no doubt things would right themselves. Anything might happen in two years. Mind, it's not your father's idea, it's mine. I'd do anything for him; he has done me many a good turn in his time, and I want to pay him back."

Miss Hartley, softening somewhat, thanked him.

"And what is two years at your time of life?" continued the captain, brightly. "Nothing. Why, I'm going away for that time as a matter of course."

"I want to go home," said Joan. "I feel that I can't breathe in this dreary place. You wouldn't like me to die, would you?"

"Certainly not," said the captain, promptly.

"You would sooner die yourself, wouldn't you?" said Joan, with a sly glance at him.

The captain said "Yes," with all the comfortable assurance of a healthy man living in a civilized country. Then he started as Miss Hartley turned suddenly and pinched his arm.

"Eh?" cried the captain, rubbing it.

"I don't want you to die for me," said Joan with a little laugh, "but I was thinking over things the other day, and I got an idea of how you could help me if you would. I gave it up, however. I felt sure you wouldn't do it, but if you say you would die for me—

"When I said 'die'—" began the captain, uneasily.

"I'm not going to ask you to do anything as dreadful as that," continued Joan; "at least, I don't think it is; but the beauty of it is it is something you can do. I am going back to Salthaven, but to make everybody comfortable and happy I thought of going back under a new name. That's the idea."

"New name?" repeated the puzzled captain.

Joan nodded and turned a somewhat flushed face in his direction.

"A new name," she repeated. "My father will be left undisturbed, Mr. John Vyner will be satisfied, and Mr. Robert—"

"Yes?" said the captain, after a pause.

"Nothing," said the girl.

"But I don't understand," said the captain, "What good will changing your name do?"

"Wait till you hear it," retorted the girl, with an amused glance at him.

"I am waiting," said the other, somewhat shortly.

"You'll see at once when I tell you," said Joan; "and I'm sure you won't mind. I am going back to Salthaven under the name of Mrs. Trimblett."

The captain stopped suddenly in his stride, and with a bewildered air strove to rally his disordered faculties. Alarm and consternation choked his utterance.

"Poor dear!" said Joan, with another giggle. "Don't be alarmed. It's the best thing that could happen to you; it will prevent all other attempts on your freedom."

"I can take a joke," said the captain, finding his speech at last; "I can take a joke as well as most men, but this is going a trifle too far."

"But I'm not joking," said the girl. "I'm going back as Mrs. Trimblett; I am, indeed. Don't look so frightened; I'm not going to marry you, really. Only pretend, as the children say."

"You don't know what you're talking about!" exclaimed the astonished captain.

"Putting aside your feelings—and mine," said Joan, "it's a good thing for everybody else, isn't it? We mustn't consider ourselves—that would be selfish."

The captain shook his head in angry amazement.

"I suppose, when you said just now that you would do anything for father, you didn't mean it, then?" said Joan. "And when you said you'd die for me, you—"

"I tell you," interrupted the captain, violently, "it's impossible. I never heard of such a thing."

"It's quite possible," declared the girl. "I shall go back home, and you must get back to Salthaven just in time to sail. Mr. Vyner will be so pleased at the news, he will let you stay away as long as you like, I am sure."

"And what about when I come back?" demanded the captain.

"When you come back," said Joan, slowly—"just before, in fact—I shall tell the truth and give people to understand that I did it to oblige you—to prevent somebody else marrying you against your will."

"Oh!" said the captain, struggling nobly with his feelings. "Oh, you will!"

"To-morrow," continued Joan, "I will buy the wedding-ring. I know that that ought to be your business, but I'll get it, because I know where I can get one cheap. I saw some the other day. Rolled gold they are called. Eighteenpence each."

The captain choked.

"Have you considered," he said, loftily, as soon as he was capable of speech, "that it would be a lie?"

Joan nodded, carelessly.

"A lie!" repeated Captain Trimblett, in a thrilling voice.

"Yes," said Joan. "I remember I heard you tell father once that if you had a sovereign for every lie you had told you would be able to give up the sea. So you had better do it. You can do it better than I can."

Captain Trimblett threw his hands apart with a sudden supreme gesture.

"I won't listen to another word!" he said, hotly. "I should never hear the end of it. Where are those omnibuses?"

"We are not near them yet," was the reply. "We have been walking away from them. When you have listened to reason I will take you to them."

The captain closed his lips obstinately. He would have closed his ears, too, if he could, but, unable to do that, quickened his pace in a forlorn attempt to outdistance her. She plied him with arguments and entreaties, but in vain. He was immovable. Finally, in a trembling voice, she said that it didn't matter, and apologized for troubling him with her concerns.

"I would do anything in reason, my dear," said the mollified captain.

"It doesn't matter," repeated the girl.

"It's quite impossible," said the captain, gently. "It's really an outrageous idea. You'll see it yourself by and by."

Miss Hartley thanked him, and taking out a handkerchief dabbed her eyes gently and made a pathetic attempt to smile.

"Don't say any more about it," she pleaded. "I have no doubt you are right. Only when you said you would do anything for us I—I thought you meant it. I see how uncomfortable it might be for you. I ought to have thought of that before."

The unfortunate captain turned crimson, but, glancing at the spectacle of resignation by his side, managed to keep his temper under restraint.

"I'm not thinking of myself at all," he growled.

"Perhaps you are without knowing it," suggested Miss Hartley, in a voice free from all trace of personal feeling. "I thought that you would have done a little thing like that for me—and father. I'm sorry I was mistaken. However, I shall go back to Salthaven in any case."

She dabbed a perfectly dry eye again, and watched the captain closely with the other.

"I suppose there will be trouble," she continued, meditatively; "still, that will be your fault. I have done all I could do."

She walked on in pained silence and paid no heed to the explanations and arguments by which the captain sought to justify his refusal. He began to get confused and rambling in his defence, and finally, to terminate an embarrassing interview, grunted out something about thinking it over. A moment later a radiant and admiring young woman was flattering him up to the skies.

"Mind, I only said I would think it over," said the captain, regarding her indignantly.

"Of course," said Joan, "I quite understand that; and you will write and break the news to father, won't you?"

"No, I'm hanged if I do," answered the captain.

"Never mind, then; I'll do it," said the girl, hastily. "I shall just write and tell him that I have changed my name to Trimblett. People have a right to change their name if they like. Lots of them do it. Make haste, you'll lose your omnibus. I shall never forget your kindness—never."

"Mind!" panted the captain, as she hurried him along, "it—isn't—settled. I am only going to think it over."

"I don't know what we should have done without you," continued Joan. "There isn't another man in the world would be so kind, I am sure. If you were only thirty or forty years younger I would marry you in reality."

"Mind!" said the captain, grasping the rail of the omnibus and pausing with his foot on the step, "I haven't—promised."

"I'll write and tell you when I've done it," said Joan. "I'll take all the responsibility. Good-by! Good-by!"

The conductor hoisted him aboard and he slowly mounted the stairs. He paused at the top to wave a feeble hand, and then, subsiding heavily into a seat, sat thinking out a long and polite letter of refusal.

CHAPTER XVII

Joan Hartley's letter to her father was not so easy to write as she had imagined. She tore up draft after draft, and at last, in despair, wrote him a brief and dutiful epistle, informing him that she had changed her name to Tremblett. She added—in a postscript—that she expected he would be surprised; and, having finished her task, sat trying to decide whether to commit it to the post or the flames.

It was a question that occupied her all the evening, and the following morning found her still undecided. It was not until the afternoon, when a letter came from Captain Trimblett, declining in violent terms and at great length to be a party to her scheme, that she made up her mind. The information that he had been recalled to Salthaven on the day following only served to strengthen her resolution, and it was with a feeling of almost pious thankfulness that she realized the advantages of such an arrangement. She went out and posted her letter to her father, and then, with a mind at ease, wrote a nice letter to Captain Trimblett, full of apologies for her precipitancy, and regretting that he had not informed her before of what she called his change of mind. She added that, after mature deliberation, she had decided not to return to Salthaven until after he had sailed.

Captain Trimblett got the letter next morning and, hurrying off to the nearest post-office, filled up a telegraph-form with a few incisive words dashed off at white heat. He destroyed six forms before he had arrived at what he considered a happy mean between strength and propriety, and then at the lady clerk's earnest request altered one of the words of the seventh. A few hours later he was on his way to Salthaven.

It was late when he arrived and the office of Vyner and Son was closed. He went on to Laurel Lodge, and, after knocking and ringing for some time in vain, walked back to the town and went on board his ship. The new crew had not yet been signed on, and Mr. Walters, the only man aboard, was cut short in his expressions of pleasure at the captain's return and sent ashore for provisions.

"Time you went to sea again," said the captain a little later as the boatswain went on his hands and knees to recover the pieces of a plate he had dropped.

"I wish I'd gone a month ago, sir," said Mr. Walters. "Shore's no place for a sailorman."

The captain grunted, and turning suddenly surprised the eye of Mr. Walters fixed upon him with an odd, puzzled expression that he had noticed before that evening. Mr. Walters, caught in the act, ducked from sight, and recovered a crumb that was trying to pass itself off as a piece of china.

"What are you staring at me for?" demanded the captain.

"Me, sir?" said the boatswain. "I wasn't staring."

He rose with his hands full of pieces and retreated to the door. Almost against his will he stole another glance at the captain and blinked hastily at the gaze that met his own.

"If I've got a smut on my nose—" began the captain, ferociously.

"No, sir," said Mr. Walters, disappearing.

"Come here!" roared the other.

The boatswain came back reluctantly.

"If I catch you making those faces at me again," said the captain, whom the events of the last day or two had reduced to a state of chronic ill-temper, "I'll—I'll—"

"Yessir," said Mr. Walters, cheerfully. "I—"

He disappeared again, but his voice came floating down the companion-ladder. "I 'ope—you'll accept—my good—wishes."

Captain Trimblett started as though he had been stung, and his temperature rose to as near boiling point as science and the human mechanism will allow. Twice he opened his mouth to bellow the boatswain back again, and twice his courage failed him. He sat a picture of wrathful consternation until, his gaze falling on a bottle of beer, he emptied it with great rapidity, and pushing his plate away and lighting his pipe sat trying to read a harmless meaning into Mr. Walters's infernal congratulations.

He rose early next morning and set off for Laurel Lodge, a prey to gloom, which the furtive glances of Mr. Walters had done nothing to dissipate. Hartley was still in his bedroom when he arrived, but Rosa showed him into the dining-room, and, having placed a chair, sped lightly upstairs.

"I've told him," she said, returning in a breathless condition and smiling at him.

The captain scowled at her.

"And he says he'll be down in a minute."

"Very good," said the captain, with a nod of dismissal.

Miss Jelks went as far as the sideboard, and, taking out a tablecloth, proceeded to set the breakfast, regarding the captain with unaffected interest as she worked.

"He ain't been very well the last day or two," she said, blandly.

The captain ignored her.

"Seems to have something on his mind," continued Miss Jelks, with a toss of her head, as she placed the sugar-bowl and other articles on the table.

The captain regarded her steadily for a moment, and then, turning, took up a newspaper.

"I should think he never was what you'd call a strong man," murmured Miss Jelks. "He ain't got the look of it."

The captain's temper got the better of him. "Who are you talking about?" he demanded, turning sharply.

Miss Jelks's eyes shone, but there was no hurry, and she smoothed down a corner of the tablecloth before replying.

"Your father-in-law, sir," she said, with a faint air of surprise.

Captain Trimblett turned hastily to his paper again, but despite his utmost efforts a faint wheezing noise escaped him and fell like soft music on the ears of Miss Jelks. In the hope that it might be repeated, or that manifestations more gratifying still might be vouchsafed to her, she lingered over her task and coughed in an aggressive fashion at intervals.

She was still busy when Hartley came downstairs, and, stopping for a moment at the doorway, stood regarding the captain with a look of timid disapproval. The latter rose and, with a significant glance in the direction of Rosa, shook hands and made a remark about the weather.

"When did you return?" inquired Hartley, trying to speak easily.

"Last night," said the other. "I came on here, but you were out."

Hartley nodded, and they sat eying each other uneasily and waiting for the industrious Rosa to go. The captain got tired first, and throwing open the French windows slipped out into the garden and motioned to Hartley to follow.

"Joan wrote to you," he said, abruptly, as soon as they were out of earshot.

"Yes," said the other, stiffly.

"Understand, it wasn't my fault," said the captain, warmly. "I wash my hands of it. I told her not to."

"Indeed!" said Hartley, with a faint attempt at sarcasm. "It was no concern of mine, of course."

The captain turned on him sharply, and for a moment scathing words hung trembling on his lips. He controlled himself by an effort.

"She wrote to you," he said, slowly, "and instead of waiting to see me, or communicating with me, you spread the news all over the place."

"Nothing of the kind," said Hartley. "As a matter of fact, it's not a thing I am anxious to talk about. Up to the present I have only told Rosa."

"Only!" repeated the choking captain. "Only! Only told Rosa! Where was the town-crier? What in the name of common-sense did you want to tell her for?"

"She would have to be told sooner or later," said Hartley, staring at him, "and it seemed to me better to tell her before Joan came home. I thought Joan would prefer it; and if you had heard Rosa's comments I think that you'd agree I was right."

The captain scarcely listened. "Well, it's all over Salthaven by now," he said, resignedly.

He seated himself on the bench with his hands hanging loosely between his knees, and tried to think. In any case he saw himself held up to ridicule, and he had a strong feeling that to tell the truth now would precipitate a crisis between Vyner and his chief clerk. The former would probably make a fairly accurate guess at the circumstances responsible for the rumour, and act accordingly. He glanced at Hartley standing awkwardly before him, and, not without a sense of self-sacrifice, resolved to accept the situation.

"Yes; Rosa had to be told," he said, philosophically. "Fate again; you can't avoid it."

Hartley took a turn or two up and down the path.

"The news came on me like a—like a thunderbolt," he said, pausing in front of the captain. "I hadn't the slightest idea of such a thing, and if I say what I think—"

"Don't!" interrupted the captain, warmly. "What's the good?"

"When were you married?" inquired the other. "Where were you married?"

"Joan made all the arrangements," said the captain, rising hastily. "Ask her."

"But—" said the astonished Hartley.

"Ask her," repeated the captain, walking toward the house and flinging the words over his shoulder. "I'm sick of it."

He led the way into the dining-room and, at the other's invitation, took a seat at the breakfast-table, and sat wondering darkly how he was to get through the two days before he sailed. Hartley, ill at ease, poured him out a cup of coffee and called his attention to the bacon-dish.

"I can't help thinking," he said, as the captain helped himself and then pushed the dish toward him— "I can't help thinking that there is something behind all this; that there is some reason for it that I don't quite understand."

The captain started. "Never mind," he said, with gruff kindness.

"But I do mind," persisted the other. "I have got an idea that it has been done for the benefit—if you can call it that—of a third person."

The captain eyed him with benevolent concern. "Nonsense," he said, uneasily. "Nothing of the kind. We never thought of you."

"I wasn't thinking of myself," said Hartley, staring; "but I know that Joan was uneasy about you, although she pretended to laugh at it. I feel sure in my own mind that she has done this to save you from Mrs. Chinnery. If it hadn't—"

He stopped suddenly as the captain, uttering a strange gasping noise, rose and stood over him. For a second or two the captain stood struggling for speech, then, stepping back with a suddenness that overturned his chair, he grabbed his cap from the sideboard and dashed out of the house. The amazed Mr. Hartley ran to the window and, with some uneasiness, saw his old friend pelting along at the rate of a good five miles an hour.

Breathing somewhat rapidly from his exertions, the captain moderated his pace after the first hundred yards, and went on his way in a state of mind pretty evenly divided between wrath and self-pity. He walked in thought with his eyes fixed on the ground, and glancing up, too late to avoid him, saw the harbour-master approaching.

Captain Trimblett, composing his features to something as near his normal expression as the time at his disposal would allow, gave a brief nod and would have passed on. He found his way, however, blocked by sixteen stone of harbour-master, while a big, red, clean-shaven face smiled at him reproachfully.

"How are you?" said Trimblett, jerkily.

The harbour-master, who was a man of few words, made no reply. He drew back a little and, regarding the captain with smiling interest, rolled his head slowly from side to side.

"Well! Well! Well!" he said at last.

Captain Trimblett drew himself up and regarded him with a glance the austerity of which would have made most men quail. It affected the harbourmaster otherwise.

"C—ck!" he said, waggishly, and drove a forefinger like a petrified sausage into the other's ribs.

The assault was almost painful, and, before the captain could recover, the harbour-master, having exhausted his stock of witticisms, both verbal and physical, passed on highly pleased with himself.

It was only a sample of what the day held in store for the captain, and before it was half over he was reduced to a condition of raging impotence. The staff of Vyner and Son turned on their stools as one man as he entered the room, and regarded him open-eyed for the short time that he remained there. Mr. Vyner, senior, greeted him almost with cordiality, and, for the second time in his experience, extended a big white hand for him to shake.

"I have heard the news, captain," he said, in extenuation.

Captain Trimblett bowed, and in response to an expression of good wishes for his future welfare managed to thank him. He made his escape as soon as possible, and, meeting Robert Vyner on the stairs, got a fleeting glance and a nod which just admitted the fact of his existence.

The most popular man in Salthaven for the time being, he spent the best part of the day on board his ship, heedless of the fact that numerous acquaintances were scouring the town in quest of him. One or two hardy spirits even ventured on board, and, leaving with some haste, bemoaned, as they went, the change wrought by matrimony in a hitherto amiable and civil-spoken mariner.

The one drop of sweetness in his cup was the news that Mrs. Chinnery was away from home for a few days, and after carefully reconnoitring from the bridge of the Indian Chief that evening he set off to visit his lodgings. He reached Tranquil Vale unmolested, and, entering the house with a rather exaggerated air of unconcern, nodded to Mr. Truefitt, who was standing on the hearthrug smoking, and hung up his cap. Mr. Truefitt, after a short pause, shook hands with him.

"She's away," he said, in a deep voice.

"She? Who?" faltered the captain.

"Susanna," replied Mr. Truefitt, in a deeper voice still.

The captain coughed and, selecting a chair with great care, slowly seated himself.

"She left you her best wishes," continued Mr. Truefitt, still standing, and still regarding him with an air of severe disapproval.

"Much obliged," murmured the captain.

"She would do it," added Mr. Truefitt, crossing to the window and staring out at the road with his back to the captain. "And she said something about a silver-plated butter-dish; but in the circumstances I said 'No.' Miss Willett thought so too."

"How is Miss Willett?" inquired the captain, anxious to change the subject.

"All things considered, she's better than might be expected," replied Mr. Truefitt, darkly.

Captain Trimblett said that he was glad to hear it, and, finding the silence becoming oppressive, inquired affectionately concerning the health of Mrs. Willett, and learned to his discomfort that she was in the same enigmatical condition as her daughter.

"And my marriage is as far off as ever," concluded Mr. Truefitt. "Some people seem to be able to get married as often as they please, and others can't get married at all."

"It's all fate," said the captain, slowly; "it's all arranged for us."

Mr. Truefitt turned and his colour rose.

"Your little affair was arranged for you, I suppose?" he said, sharply.

"It was," said the captain, with startling vehemence.

Mr. Truefitt, who was lighting his pipe, looked up at him from lowered brows, and then, crossing to the door, took his pipe down the garden to the summer-house.

CHAPTER XVIII

"This time to-morrow night," said Mr. Walters, as he slowly paced a country lane with Miss Jelks clinging to his arm, "I shall be at sea."

Miss Jelks squeezed his arm and gave vent to a gentle sigh. "Two years'll soon slip away," she remarked. "It's wonderful how time flies. How much is twice three hundred and sixty-five?"

"And you mind you behave yourself," said the boatswain, hastily. "Remember your promise, mind."

"Of course I will," said Rosa, carelessly.

"You've promised not to 'ave your evening out till I come back," the boatswain reminded her; "week-days and Sundays both. And it oughtn't to be no 'ardship to you. Gals wot's going to be married don't want to go gadding about."

"Of course they don't," said Rosa. "I shouldn't enjoy being out without you neither. And I can get all the fresh air I want in the garden."

"And cleaning the winders," said the thoughtful boatswain.

Miss Jelks, who held to a firm and convenient belief in the likeness between promises and piecrusts, smiled cheerfully.

"Unless I happen to be sent on an errand I sha'n't put my nose outside the front gate," she declared.

"You've passed your word," said Mr. Walters, slowly, "and that's good enough for me; besides which I've got a certain party wot's promised to keep 'is eye on you and let me know if you don't keep to it."

"Eh?" said the startled Rosa. "Who is it?"

"Never you mind who it is," said Mr. Walters, judicially. "It's better for you not to know, then you can't dodge 'im. He can keep his eye on you, but there's no necessity for you to keep your eye on 'im. I don't mind wot he does."

Miss Jelks maintained her temper with some difficulty; but the absolute necessity of discovering the identity of the person referred to by Mr. Walters, if she was to have any recreation at all during the next two years, helped her.

"He'll have an easy job of it," she said, at last, with a toss of her head.

"That's just wot I told 'im," said the boatswain. "He didn't want to take the job on at first, but I p'inted out that if you behaved yourself and kept your promise he'd 'ave nothing to do; and likewise, if you didn't, it was only right as 'ow I should know. Besides which I gave 'im a couple o' carved peach stones and a war-club that used to belong to a Sandwich Islander, and took me pretty near a week to make."

Miss Jelks looked up at him sideways. "Be a bit of all right if he comes making up to me himself," she said, with a giggle. "I wonder whether he'd tell you that?"

"He won't do that," said the boatswain, with a confident smile. "He's much too well-behaved, 'sides which he ain't old enough."

Miss Jelks tore her arm away. "You've never been and set that old-fashioned little shrimp Bassett on to watch me?" she said, shrilly.

"Never you mind who it is," growled the discomfited boatswain. "It's got nothing to do with you. All you've got to know is this: any time 'e sees you out—this party I'm talking of—he's going to log it. He calls it keeping a dairy, but it comes to the same thing."

"I know what I call it," said the offended maiden, "and if I catch that little horror spying on me he'll remember it."

"He can't spy on you if you ain't out," said the boatswain. "That's wot I told 'im; and when I said as you'd promised he saw as 'ow it would be all right. I'm going to try and bring him 'ome a shark's tooth."

"Goin' to make it?" inquired Rosa, with a sniff.

"And might I ask," she inquired, as the amorous boatswain took her arm again, "might I ask who is going to watch you?"

"Me?" said the boatswain, regarding her with honest amazement. "I don't want no watching. Men don't."

"Indeed!" said Miss Jelks, "and why not?"

"They don't like it," said Mr. Walters, simply.

Miss Jelks released her arm again, and for some time they walked on opposite sides of the lane Her temper rose rapidly, and at last, tearing off her glove, she drew the ring from her finger and handed it to the boatswain.

"There you are!" she exclaimed. "Take it!"

Mr. Walters took it, and, after a vain attempt to place it on his little finger, put it in his waistcoat-pocket and walked on whistling.

"We're not engaged now," explained Rosa.

"Aye, aye," said the boatswain, cheerfully. "Only walking out."

"Nothing of the kind," said Rosa. "I sha'n't have nothing more to do with you. You'd better tell Bassett."

"What for?" demanded the other.

"What for?" repeated Rosa. "Why, there's no use him watching me now."

"Why not?" demanded Mr. Walters.

Miss Jelks caught her breath impatiently. "Because it's got nothing to do with you what I do now," she said, sharply. "I can go out with who I like."

"Ho!" said the glaring Mr. Walters. "Ho! Can you? So that's your little game, is it? Here—"

He fumbled in his pocket and, producing the ring, caught Miss Jelks's hand in a grip that made her wince, and proceeded to push it on her little finger. "Now you behave yourself, else next time I'll take it back for good."

Miss Jelks remonstrated, but in vain. The boatswain passed his left arm about her waist, and when she became too fluent increased the pressure until she gasped for breath. Much impressed by these signs of affection she began to yield, and, leaning her head against his shoulder, voluntarily renewed her vows of seclusion.

She went down to the harbour next day to see him off, and stood watching with much interest the bustle on deck and the prominent share borne by her masterful admirer. To her thinking, Captain Trimblett, stiff and sturdy on the bridge, played but a secondary part. She sent the boatswain little signals of approval and regard, a proceeding which was the cause of much subsequent trouble to a newly joined A.B. who misunderstood their destination. The warps were thrown off, a bell clanged in the engine-room, the screw revolved, and a gradually widening piece of water appeared between the steamer and the quay. Men on board suspended work for a moment for a last gaze ashore, and no fewer than six unfortunates responded ardently to the fluttering of her handkerchief. She stood watching until the steamer had disappeared round a bend in the river, and then, with a sense of desolation and a holiday feeling for which there was no outlet, walked slowly home.

She broke her promise to the boatswain the following evening. For one thing, it was her "evening out," and for another she felt that the sooner the Bassett nuisance was stopped, the better it would be for all concerned. If the youth failed to see her she was the gainer to the extent of an evening in the open air, and if he did not she had an idea that the emergency would not find her unprepared.

She walked down to the town first and spent some time in front of the shop-windows. Tiring of this, she proceeded to the harbour and inspected the shipping, and then with the feeling strong upon her that it would be better to settle with Bassett at her own convenience, she walked slowly to the small street in which he lived, and taking up a position nearly opposite his house paced slowly to and fro with the air of one keeping an appointment. She was pleased to observe, after a time, a slight movement of the curtains opposite, and, satisfied that she had attained her ends, walked off. The sound of a street door closing saved her the necessity of looking round.

At first she strolled slowly through the streets, but presently, increasing her pace, resolved to take the lad for a country walk. At Tranquil Vale she paused to tie up her boot-lace, and, satisfying herself that Bassett was still in pursuit, set off again.

She went on a couple of miles farther, until turning the sharp corner of a lane she took a seat on the trunk of a tree that lay by the side and waited for him to come up. She heard his footsteps coming nearer and nearer, and with a satisfied smile noted that he had quickened his pace. He came round the corner at the rate of over four miles an hour, and, coming suddenly upon her, was unable to repress a slight exclamation of surprise. The check was but momentary, and he was already passing on when the voice of Miss Jelks, uplifted in sorrow, brought him to a standstill.

"Oh, Master Bassett," she cried, "I am surprised! I couldn't have believed it of you."

Bassett, squeezing his hands together, stood eying her nervously.

"And you so quiet, too," continued Rosa; "but there, you quiet ones are always the worst."

The boy, peering at her through his spectacles, made no reply.

"The idea of a boy your age falling in love with me," said Rosa, modestly lowering her gaze.

"What!" squeaked the astonished Bassett, hardly able to believe his ears.

"Falling in love and dogging my footsteps," said Rosa, with relish, "and standing there looking at me as though you could eat me."

"You must be mad," said Bassett, in a trembling voice. "Stark staring mad."

"It's to make you leave off loving me," she explained

"Don't make it worse," said Rosa kindly. "I suppose you can't help it, and ought to be pitied for it really. Now I know why it was you winked at me when you came to the house the other day."

"Winked!" gasped the horrified youth. "Me?"

"I thought it was weakness of sight, at the time," said the girl, "but I see my mistake now. I am sorry for you, but it can never be. I am another's."

Bassett, utterly bereft of speech, stood eying her helplessly.

"Don't stand there making those sheep's eyes at me," said Rosa. "Try and forget me. Was it love at first sight, or did it come on gradual like?"

Bassett, moistening his tongue, shook his head.

"Am I the first girl you ever loved?" inquired Rosa, softly.

"No," said the boy. "I mean—I have never been in—love. I don't know what you are talking about."

"Do you mean to say you are not in love with me?" demanded Rosa, springing up suddenly.

"I do," said Bassett, blushing hotly.

"Then what did you follow me all round the town for, and then down here?"

Bassett, who was under a pledge of secrecy to the boatswain, and, moreover, had his own ideas as to the reception the truth might meet with, preserved an agonized silence.

"It's no good," said Rosa, eying him mournfully. "You can't deceive me. You are head over heels, and the kindest thing I can do is to be cruel to you—for your own sake."

She sprang forward suddenly, and, before the astounded youth could dodge, dealt him a sharp box on the ear. As he reeled under the blow she boxed the other.

"It's to make you leave off loving me," she explained; "and if I ever catch you following me again you'll get some more; besides which I shall tell your mother."

She picked up her parasol from the trunk, and after standing regarding him for a moment with an air of offended maidenhood, walked back to the town. Bassett, after a long interval, returned by another road.

CHAPTER XIX

Joan Harltey returned to Salthaven a week after Captain Trimblett's departure, and, with a lively sense of her inability to satisfy the curiosity of her friends, spent most of the time indoors. To evade her father's inquiries she adopted other measures, and the day after her return, finding both her knowledge and imagination inadequate to the task of satisfying him, she first waxed impatient and then tearful. Finally she said that she was thoroughly tired of the subject, and expressed a fervent hope that she might hear no more about it. Any further particulars would be furnished by Captain Trimblett, upon his return.

"But when I asked him about it he referred me to you," said Hartley. "The whole affair is most incomprehensible."

"We thought it would be a surprise to you," agreed Joan.

"It was," said her father, gloomily. "But if you are satisfied, I suppose it is all right."

He returned to the attack next day, but gained little information. Miss Hartley's ideas concerning the various marriage ceremonies were of the vaguest, but by the aid of "Whitaker's Almanack" she was enabled to declare that the marriage had taken place by license at a church in the district where Trimblett was staying. As a help to identification she added that the church was built of stone, and that the pew-opener had a cough. Tiresome questions concerning the marriage certificate were disposed of by leaving it in the captain's pocket-book. And again she declared that she was tired of the subject.

"I can't imagine what your aunt was thinking about," said her father. "If you had let me write—"

"She knew nothing about it," said Joan, hastily; "and if you had written to her she would have thought that you were finding fault with her for not looking after me more. It's done now, and if I'm satisfied and Captain Trimblett is satisfied, that is all that matters. You didn't want me to be an old maid, did you?"

Mr. Hartley gave up the subject in despair, but Miss Willett, who called a day or two later, displayed far more perseverance. After the usual congratulations she sat down to discuss the subject at length, and subjected Joan to a series of questions which the latter had much difficulty in evading. For a newly married woman, Miss Willett could only regard her knowledge of matrimony as hazy in the extreme.

"She don't want to talk about it," said Mr. Truefitt, the following evening as he sat side by side with Miss Willett in the little summer-house overlooking the river. "Perhaps she is repenting it already."

"It ought to be a tender memory," sighed Miss Willett. "I'm sure—"

She broke off and blushed.

"Yes?" said Mr. Truefitt, pinching her arm tenderly.

"Never mind," breathed Miss Willett. "I mean—I was only going to say that I don't think the slightest detail would have escaped me. All she seems to remember is that it took place in a church."

"It must have been by license, I should think," said Mr. Truefitt, scowling thoughtfully. "Ordinary license, I should say. I have been reading up about them lately. One never knows what may happen."

Miss Willett started.

"Trimblett has not behaved well," continued Mr. Truefitt, slowly, "by no means, but I must say that he has displayed a certain amount of dash; he didn't allow anything or anybody to come between him and matrimony. He just went and did it."

He passed his arm round Miss Willett's waist and gazed reflectively across the river.

"And I suppose we shall go on waiting all our lives," he said at last. "We consider other people far too much."

Miss Willett shook her head. "Mother always keeps to her word," she said, with an air of mournful pride. "Once she says anything she keeps to it. That's her firmness. She won't let me marry so long as Mrs. Chinnery stays here. We must be patient."

Mr. Truefitt rumpled his hair irritably and for some time sat silent. Then he leaned forward and, in a voice trembling with excitement, whispered in the lady's ear.

"Peter!" gasped Miss Willett, and drew back and eyed him in trembling horror.

"Why not?" said Mr. Truefitt, with an effort to speak stoutly. "It's our affair."

Miss Willett shivered and, withdrawing from his arm, edged away to the extreme end of the seat and averted her gaze.

"It's quite easy," whispered the tempter.

Miss Willett, still looking out at the door, affected not to hear.

"Not a soul would know until afterward," continued Mr. Truefitt, in an ardent whisper. "It could all be kept as quiet as possible. I'll have the license ready, and you could just slip out for a morning walk and meet me at the church, and there you are. And it's ridiculous of two people of our age to go to such trouble."

"Mother would never forgive me," murmured Miss Willett. "Never!"

"She'd come round in time," said Mr. Truefitt.

"Never!" said Miss Willett. "You don't know mother's strength of mind. But I mustn't stay and listen to such things. It's wicked!"

She got up and slipped into the garden, and with Mr. Truefitt in attendance paced up and down the narrow paths.

"Besides," she said, after a long silence, "I shouldn't like to share housekeeping with your sister. It would only lead to trouble between us, I am sure."

Mr. Truefitt came to a halt in the middle of the path, and stood rumpling his hair again as an aid to thought. Captain Sellers, who was looking over his fence, waved a cheery salutation.

"Fine evening," he piped.

The other responded with a brief nod.

"What did you say?" inquired Captain Sellers, who was languishing for a little conversation.

"Didn't say anything!" bawled Mr. Truefitt.

"You must speak up if you want me to hear you!" cried the captain. "It's one o' my bad days."

Truefitt shook his head, and placing himself by the side of Miss Willett resumed his walk. Three fences away, Captain Sellers kept pace with them.

"Nothing fresh about Trimblett, I suppose?" he yelled.

Truefitt shook his head again.

"He's a deep 'un!" cried Sellers—"wonderful deep! How's the other one? Bearing up? I ain't seen her about the last day or two. I believe that was all a dodge of Trimblett's to put us off the scent. It made a fool of me."

Mr. Truefitt, with a nervous glance at the open windows of his house, turned and walked hastily down the garden again.

"He quite deceived me," continued Captain Sellers, following—"quite. What did you say?"

"Nothing," bawled Mr. Truefitt, with sudden ferocity.

"Eh!" yelled the captain, leaning over the fence with his hand to his ear.

"Nothing!"

"Eh?" said the captain, anxiously. "Speak up! What?"

"Oh, go to—Jericho!" muttered Mr. Truefitt, and, taking Miss Willett by the arm, disappeared into the summer-house again. "Where were we when that old idiot interrupted us?" he inquired, tenderly.

Miss Willett told him, and, nestling within his encircling arm, listened with as forbidding an expression as she could command to further arguments on the subject of secret marriages.

"It's no use," she said at last "I mustn't listen. It's wicked. I am surprised at you, Peter. You must never speak to me on the subject again."

She put her head on his shoulder, and Mr. Truefitt, getting a better grip with his arm, drew her toward him.

"Think it over," he whispered, and bent and kissed her.

"Never," was the reply.

Mr. Truefitt kissed her again, and was about to repeat the performance when she started up with a faint scream, and, pushing him away, darted from the summer-house and fled up the garden. Mr. Truefitt, red with wrath, stood his ground and stared ferociously at the shrunken figure of Captain Sellers standing behind the little gate in the fence that gave on to the foreshore. The captain, with a cheery smile, lifted the latch and entered the garden.

"I picked a little bunch o' flowers for Miss Willett," he said, advancing and placing them on the table.

"Who told you to come into my garden?" shouted the angry Mr. Truefitt.

"Yes, all of 'em," said Captain Sellers, taking up the bunch and looking at them. "Smell!"

He thrust the bunch into the other's face, and withdrawing it plunged his own face into it with rapturous sniffs. Mr. Truefitt, his nose decorated with pollen ravished from a huge lily, eyed him murderously.

"Get out of my garden," he said, with an imperious wave of his hand.

"I can't hear what you say," said the captain, following the direction of the other's hand and stepping outside. "Sometimes I think my deafness gets worse. It's a great deprivation."

"Is it?" said Mr. Truefitt. He made a funnel of both hands and bent to the old man's willing ear.

"You're an artful, interfering, prying, inquisitive old busybody," he bellowed. "Can you hear that?"

"Say it again," said the captain, his old eyes snapping.

Mr. Truefitt complied.

"I didn't quite catch the last word," said the captain.

"Busybody!" yelled Mr. Truefitt. "Busybody! B—u—s—"

"I heard," said Captain Sellers, with sudden and alarming dignity. "Take your coat off."

"Get out of my garden," responded Mr. Truefitt, briefly.

"Take your coat off," repeated Captain Sellers, sternly. He removed his own after a little trouble, and rolling back his shirt sleeves stood regarding with some pride a pair of yellow, skinny old arms. Then he clenched his fists, and, with an agility astonishing in a man of his years, indulged in a series of galvanic little hops in front of the astounded Peter Truefitt.

"Put your hands up!" he screamed. "Put 'em up, you tailor's dummy! Put 'em up, you Dutchman!"

"Go out of my garden," repeated the marvelling Mr. Truefitt. "Go home and have some gruel and go to bed!"

Captain Sellers paid no heed. Still performing marvellous things with his feet, he ducked his head over one shoulder, feinted with his left at Mr. Truefitt's face, and struck with his right somewhere near the centre of his opponent's waistcoat. Mr. Truefitt, still gazing at him open-mouthed, retreated backward, and, just as the captain's parchment-like fist struck him a second time, tripped over a water-can that had been left in the path and fell heavily on his back in a flower-bed.

"Time!" cried Captain Sellers, breathlessly, and pulled out a big silver watch to consult, as Miss Willett came hurrying down the garden, followed by Mrs. Chinnery.

"Peter!" wailed Miss Willett, going on her knees and raising his head. "Oh, Peter!"

"Has he hurt you?" inquired Mrs. Chinnery, stooping.

"No; I'm a bit shaken," said Mr. Truefitt, crossly. "I fell over that bla—blessed water-can. Take that old marionette away. I'm afraid to touch him for fear he'll fall to pieces."

"Time!" panted Captain Sellers, stowing his watch away and resuming his prancing. "Come on! Lively with it!"

Miss Willett uttered a faint scream and thrust her hand out.

"Lor' bless the man!" cried Mrs. Chinnery, regarding the old gentleman's antics with much amazement "Go away! Go away at once!"

"Time!" cried Captain Sellers.

She stepped forward, and her attitude was so threatening that Captain Sellers hesitated. Then he turned, and, picking up his coat, began to struggle into it.

"I hope it will be a lesson to him," he said, glaring at Mr. Truefitt, who had risen by this time and was feeling his back. "You see what comes of insulting an old sea-dog."

He turned and made his way to the gate, refusing with a wave of his hand Mrs. Chinnery's offer to help him down the three steps leading to the shore. With head erect and a springy step he gained his own garden, and even made a pretence of attending to a flower or two before sitting down. Then the deck-chair claimed him, and he lay, a limp bundle of aching old bones, until his housekeeper came down the garden to see what had happened to him.

CHAPTER XX

For the first week or two after Joan Hartley's return Mr. Robert Vyner went about in a state of gloomy amazement. Then, the first shock of surprise over, he began to look about him in search of reasons for a marriage so undesirable. A few casual words with Hartley at odd times only served to deepen the mystery, and he learned with growing astonishment of the chief clerk's ignorance of the whole affair. A faint suspicion, which he had at first dismissed as preposterous, persisted in recurring to him, and grew in strength every time the subject was mentioned between them. His spirits improved, and he began to speak of the matter so cheerfully that Hartley became convinced that everybody concerned had made far too much of ordinary attentions paid by an ordinary young man to a pretty girl. Misled by his son's behaviour, Mr. Vyner, senior, began to entertain the same view of the affair.

"Just a boyish admiration," he said to his wife, as they sat alone one evening. "All young men go through it at some time or other. It's a sort of—ha—vaccination, and the sooner they have it and get over it the better."

"He has quite got over it, I think," said Mrs. Vyner, slowly.

Mr. Vyner nodded. "Lack of opposition," he said, with a satisfied air. "Lack of visible opposition, at any rate. These cases require management. Many a marriage has been caused by the efforts made to prevent it."

Mrs. Vyner sighed. Her husband had an irritating habit of taking her a little way into his confidence and then leaving the rest to an imagination which was utterly inadequate to the task.

"There is nothing like management," she said, safely. "And I am sure nobody could have had a better son. He has never caused us a day's anxiety."

"Not real anxiety," said her husband—"no."

Mrs. Vyner averted her eyes. "When," she said, gently—"when are you going to give him a proper interest in the firm?"

Mr. Vyner thrust his hands into his trousers pockets and leaned back in his chair. "I have been thinking about it," he said, slowly. "He would have had it before but for this nonsense. Nothing was arranged at first, because I wanted to see how he was going to do. His work is excellent—excellent."

It was high praise, but it was deserved, and Mr. Robert Vyner would have been the first to admit it. His monstrous suspicion was daily growing less monstrous and more plausible. It became almost a conviction, and he resolved to test it by seeing Joan and surprising her with a few sudden careless remarks of the kind that a rising K.C. might spring upon a particularly difficult witness. For various reasons he chose an afternoon when the senior partner was absent, and, after trying in vain to think out a few embarrassing questions on the way, arrived at the house in a condition of mental bankruptcy.

The obvious agitation of Miss Hartley as she shook hands did not tend to put him at his ease. He stammered something about "congratulations" and the girl stammered something about "thanks," after which they sat still and eyed each other nervously.

"Beautiful day," said Mr. Vyner at last, and comforted himself with the reflection that the most eminent K.C.'s often made inane remarks with the idea of throwing people off their guard.

Miss Hartley said "Yes."

"I hope you had a nice time in town?" he said, suddenly.

"Very nice," said Joan, eying him demurely.

"But of course you did," said Robert, with an air of sudden remembrance. "I suppose Captain Trimblett knows London pretty well?"

"Pretty well," repeated the witness.

Mr. Vyner eyed her thoughtfully. "I hope you won't mind my saying so," he said, slowly, "but I was awfully pleased to hear of your marriage. I think it is always nice to hear of one's friends marrying each other."

"Yes," said the girl.

"And Trimblett is such a good chap," continued Mr. Vyner. "He is so sensible for his age."

He paused expectantly, but nothing happened.

"So bright and cheerful," he explained.

Miss Hartley still remaining silent, he broke off and sat watching her quietly. To his eyes she seemed more charming than ever. There was a defiant look in her eyes, and a half-smile trembled round the corners of her mouth. He changed his seat for one nearer to hers, and leaning forward eyed her gravely. Her colour deepened and she breathed quickly.

"Don't—don't you think Captain Trimblett is lucky?" she inquired, with an attempt at audacity.

Mr. Vyner pondered. "No," he said at last.

Miss Hartley caught her breath.

"How rude!" she said, after a pause, lowering her eyes.

"No, it isn't," said Robert.

"Really!" remonstrated Miss Hartley.

"I think that I am luckier than he is," said Robert, in a low voice. "At least, I hope so. Shall I tell you why?"

"No," said Joan, quickly.

Mr. Vyner moistened his lips.

"Perhaps you know," he said, unsteadily.

Joan made no reply.

"You do know," said Robert.

Miss Hartley looked up with a sudden, careless laugh.

"It sounds like a conundrum," she said, gayly. "But it doesn't matter. I hope you will be lucky."

"I intend to be," said Robert.

"My hus—husband," said Joan, going very red, "would probably use the word 'fate' instead of 'luck.'"

"It is a favourite word of my wife's," said Robert gravely. "Ah, what a couple they would have made!"

"Who?" inquired Joan, eying him in bewilderment.

"My wife and your husband," said Robert. "I believe they were made for each other."

Miss Hartley retreated in good order. "I think you are talking nonsense," she said, with some dignity.

"Yes," said Robert, with a smile. "Ground-bait."

"What?" said Joan, in a startled voice.

"Ground-bait."

Miss Hartley made an appeal to his better feelings. "You are making my head ache," she said, pathetically. "I'm sure I don't know what you are talking about."

Mr. Vyner apologized, remarking that it was a common fault of young husbands to talk too much about their wives, and added, as an interesting fact, that he had only been married that afternoon. Miss Hartley turned a deaf ear.

He spread a little ground-bait—of a different kind—before Hartley during the next few days, and in a short time had arrived at a pretty accurate idea of the state of affairs. It was hazy and lacking in detail, but it was sufficient to make him give Laurel Lodge a wide berth for the time being, and to work still harder for that share in the firm which he had always been given to understand would be his. In the meantime he felt that Joan's marriage de convenance was a comfortable arrangement for all parties concerned.

This was still his view of it as he sat in his office one afternoon about a couple of months after Captain Trimblett's departure. He had met Miss Hartley in the street the day before, and, with all due regard to appearances, he could not help thinking that she had been somewhat unnecessarily demure. In return she had gone away with three crushed fingers and a colour that was only partially due to exercise. He was leaning back in his chair thinking it over when his father entered.

"Busy?" inquired John Vyner.

"Frightfully," said his son, unclasping his hands from the back of his head.

"I have just been speaking to Hartley," said the senior partner, watching him keenly. "I had a letter this morning from the Trimblett family."

"Eh?" said his son, staring.

"From the eldest child—a girl named Jessie," replied the other. "It appears that a distant cousin who has been in charge of them has died suddenly, and she is rather at a loss what to do. She wrote to me about sending the captain's pay to her."

"Yes," said his son, nodding; "but what has Hartley got to do with it?"

"Do with it?" repeated Mr. Vyner in surprised tones. "I take it that he is in a way their grandfather."

"Gran—" began his son, and sat gasping. "Yes, of course," he said, presently, "of course. I hadn't thought of that. Of course."

"From his manner at first Hartley appeared to have forgotten it too," said Mr. Vyner, "but he soon saw with me that the children ought not to be left alone. The eldest is only seventeen."

Robert tried to collect his thoughts. "Yes," he said, slowly.

"He has arranged for them to come and live with him," continued Mr. Vyner.

The upper part of his son's body disappeared with startling suddenness over the arm of his chair and a hand began groping blindly in search of a fallen pen. A dangerous rush of blood to the head was perceptible as he regained the perpendicular.

"Was—was Hartley agreeable to that?" he inquired, steadying his voice.

His father drew himself up in his chair. "Certainly," he said, stiffly; "he fell in with the suggestion at once. It ought to have occurred to him first. Besides the relationship, he and Trimblett are old friends. The captain is an old servant of the firm and his children must be looked after; they couldn't be left alone in London."

"It's a splendid idea," said Robert—"splendid. By far the best thing that you could have done."

"I have told him to write to the girl to-night," said Mr. Vyner. "He is not sure that she knows of her father's second marriage. And I have told him to take a day or two off next week and go up to town and fetch them. It will be a little holiday for him."

"Quite a change for him," agreed Robert. Conscious of his father's scrutiny, his face was absolutely unmoved and his voice easy. "How many children are there?"

"Five," was the reply—"so she says in the letter. The two youngest are twins."

For the fraction of a second something flickered across the face of Robert Vyner and was gone.

"Trimblett's second marriage was rather fortunate for them," he said, in a matter-of-fact voice.

He restrained his feelings until his father had gone, and then, with a gasp of relief, put his head on the table and gave way to them. Convulsive tremours assailed him, and hilarious sobs escaped at intervals from his tortured frame. Ejaculations of "Joan!" and "Poor girl!" showed that he was not entirely bereft of proper feeling.

His head was still between his arms upon the table and his body still shaking, when the door opened and Bassett entered the room and stood gazing at him in a state of mild alarm. He stood for a minute diagnosing the case, and then, putting down a handful of papers, crossed softly to the mantel-piece and filled a tumbler with water. He came back and touched the junior partner respectfully on the elbow.

"Will you try and drink some of this, sir?" he said, soothingly.

The startled Robert threw up his arm. There was a crash of glass, and Bassett, with his legs apart and the water streaming down his face, stood regarding him with owlish consternation. His idea that the junior partner was suffering from a species of fit was confirmed by the latter suddenly snatching his hat from its peg and darting wildly from the room.

CHAPTER XXI

Mrs. Willett sat in her small and over-furnished living-room in a state of open-eyed amazement. Only five minutes before she had left the room to look for a pair of shoes whose easiness was their sole reason for survival, and as a last hope had looked under Cecilia's bed, and discovered the parcels.

Three parcels all done up in brown paper and ready for the post, addressed in Cecilia's handwriting to:—

Mrs. P. Truefitt,

Findlater's Private Hotel,

Finsbury Circus, London.

She smoothed her cap-strings down with trembling hands and tried to think. The autumn evening was closing in, but she made no attempt to obtain a light. Her mind was becoming active, and the shadows aided thought. At ten o'clock her daughter, returning from Tranquil Vale, was surprised to find her still sitting in the dark.

"Why, haven't you had any supper?" she inquired, lighting the gas.

"I didn't want any," said her mother, blinking at die sudden light.

Miss Willett turned and pulled down the blinds. Then she came back, and, standing behind her mother's chair, placed a hand upon her shoulder.

"It—it will be lonely for you when I've gone, mother," she said, smoothing the old lady's lace collar.

"Gone?" repeated Mrs. Willett. "Gone? Why, has that woman consented to go at last?"

Miss Willett shrank back. "No," she said, trembling, "but—"

"You can't marry till she does," said Mrs. Willett, gripping the arms of her chair. "Not with my consent, at any rate. Remember that. I'm not going to give way; she must."

Miss Willett said "Yes, mother," in a dutiful voice, and then, avoiding her gaze, took a few biscuits from the sideboard.

"There's a difference between strength of mind and obstinacy," continued Mrs. Willett. "It's obstinacy with her—sheer obstinacy; and I am not going to bow down to it—there's no reason why I should."

Miss Willett said "No, mother."

"If other people like to bow down to her," said Mrs. Willett, smoothing her dress over her knees, "that's their look-out. But she won't get me doing it."

She went up to bed and lay awake half the night, and, rising late next morning in consequence, took advantage of her daughter's absence to peer under the bed. The parcels had disappeared. She went downstairs, with her faded but alert old eyes watching Cecilia's every movement.

"When does Mr. Truefitt begin his holidays?" she inquired, at last.

Miss Willett, who had been glancing restlessly at the clock, started violently.

"To—to—to-day," she gasped.

Mrs. Willett said "Oh!"

"I—I was going out with him at eleven—for a little walk," said her daughter, nervously. "Just a stroll."

Mrs. Willett nodded. "Do you good," she said, slowly. "What are you going to wear?"

Her daughter, still trembling, looked at her in surprise. "This," she said, touching her plain brown dress.

Mrs. Willett's voice began to tremble. "It's—it's rather plain," she said. "I like my daughter to be nicely dressed, especially when she is going out with her future husband. Go upstairs and put on your light green."

Miss Willett, paler than ever, gave a hasty and calculating glance at the clock and disappeared.

"And your new hat," Mrs. Willett called after her.

She looked at the clock too, and then, almost as excited as her daughter, began to move restlessly about the room. Her hands shook, and going up to the glass over the mantel-piece she removed her spectacles and dabbed indignantly at her eyes. By the time Cecilia returned she was sitting in her favourite chair, a picture of placid and indifferent old age.

"That's better," she said, with an approving nod; "much better."

She rose, and going up to her daughter rearranged her dress a little. "You look very nice, dear," she paid, with a little cough. "Mr. Truefitt ought to be proud of you. Good-by."

Her daughter kissed her, and then, having got as far as the door, came back and kissed her again. She made a second attempt to depart, and then, conscience proving too much for her, uttered a stifled sob and came back to her mother.

"Oh, I can't," she wailed; "I can't."

"You'll be late," said her mother, pushing her away. "Good-by."

"I can't," sobbed Miss Willett; "I can't do it. I'm—I'm deceiving—"

"Yes, yes," said the old lady, hastily; "tell me another time. Good-by."

She half led and half thrust her daughter to the door.

"But," said the conscience-stricken Cecilia, "you don't under—"

"A walk will do you good," said her mother; "and don't cry; try and look your best."

She managed to close the door on her, and her countenance cleared as she heard her daughter open the hall door and pass out. Standing well back in the room, she watched her to the gate, uttering a sharp exclamation of annoyance as Cecilia, with a woebegone shake of the head, turned and came up the path again. A loud tap at the window and a shake of the head were necessary to drive her off.

Mrs. Willett gave her a few minutes' start, and then, in a state of extraordinary excitement, went upstairs and, with fingers trembling with haste, put on her bonnet and cape.

"You're not going out alone at this time o' the morning, ma'am?" said the old servant, as she came down again.

"Just as far as the corner, Martha," said the old lady, craftily.

"I'd better come with you," said the other.

"Certainly not," said Mrs. Willett. "I'm quite strong this morning. Go on with your stoves."

She took up her stick and, opening the door, astonished Martha by her nimbleness. At the gate she looked right and left, and for the first time in her life felt that there were too many churches in Salthaven. For several reasons, the chief being that Cecilia's father lay in the churchyard, she decided to try St. Peter's first, and, having procured a cab at the end of the road, instructed the cabman to drive to within fifty yards of the building and wait for her.

The church was open, and a peep through the swing-doors showed her a small group standing before the altar. With her hand on her side she hobbled up the stone steps to the gallery, and, helping herself along by the sides of the pews, entered the end one of them all and sank exhausted on the cushions.

The service had just commenced, and the voice of the minister sounded with unusual loudness in the empty church. Mr. Truefitt and Miss Willett stood before him like culprits, Mr. Truefitt glancing round uneasily several times as the service proceeded. Twice the old lavender-coloured bonnet that was projecting over the side of the gallery drew back in alarm, and twice its owner held her breath and rated herself sternly for her venturesomeness. She did not look over again until she heard a little clatter of steps proceeding to the vestry, and then, with a hasty glance round, slipped out of the pew and made her way downstairs and out of the church.

Her strength was nearly spent, but the cabman was on the watch, and, driving up to the entrance, climbed down and bundled her into the cab. The drive was all too short for her to compose herself as she would have liked, and she met the accusatory glance of Martha with but little of her old spirit.

"I went a little too far," she said, feebly, as the servant helped her to the door.

"What did I tell you?" demanded the other, and placing her in her chair removed her bonnet and cape, and stood regarding her with sour disapproval.

"I'm getting better," said the old lady, stoutly.

"I'm getting my breath back again. I—I think I'll have a glass of wine."

"Yes, 'm," said Martha, moving off. "The red-currant?"

"Red-currant!" said Mrs. Willett, sharply. "Red-currant! Certainly not. The port."

Martha disappeared, marvelling, to return a minute or two later with the wine and a glass on a tray. Mrs. Willett filled her glass and, whispering a toast to herself, half emptied it.

"Martha!" she said, looking round with a smile.

"Ma'am!"

"If you like to go and get a glass you can have a little drop yourself."

She turned and took up her glass again, and, starting nervously, nearly let it fall as a loud crash sounded outside. The bewildered Martha had fallen downstairs.

CHAPTER XXII

Joan Harltey did not realize the full consequences of her departure from the truth until the actual arrival of the Trimblett family, which, piloted by Mr. Hartley, made a triumphant appearance in a couple of station cabs. The roofs were piled high with luggage, and the leading cabman shared his seat with a brass-bound trunk of huge dimensions and extremely sharp corners.

A short, sturdy girl of seventeen jumped out as soon as the vehicles came to a halt, and, taking her stand on the curb, proceeded to superintend the unloading. A succession of hasty directions to the leading cabman, one of the most docile of men, ended in the performance of a marvellous piece of jugglery with the big trunk, which he first balanced for an infinitesimal period of time on his nose, and then caught with his big toe.

"What did you do that for?" demanded Miss Trimblett, hotly.

There is a limit to the patience of every man, and the cabman was proceeding to tell her when he was checked by Mr. Hartley.

"He ought to be locked up," said Miss Trimblett flushing.

She took up a band-box and joined the laden procession of boys and girls that was proceeding up the path to the house. Still red with indignation she was introduced to Joan, and, putting down the band-box, stood eying her with frank curiosity.

"I thought you were older," she said at last. "I had no idea father was married again until I got the letter. I shall call you Joan."

"You had all better call me that," said Miss Hartley, hastily.

"Never more surprised in my life," continued Miss Trimblett. "However—"

She paused and looked about her.

"This is George," she said, pulling forward a heavy-looking youth of sixteen. "This is Ted; he is fourteen—small for his age—and these are the twins, Dolly and Gertrude; they're eleven. Dolly has got red hair and Gerty has got the sweetest temper."

The family, having been introduced and then summarily dismissed by the arbitrary Jessie, set out on a tour of inspection, while the elders, proceeding upstairs, set themselves to solve a problem in sleeping accommodation that would have daunted the proprietor of a Margate lodging-house. A scheme was at last arranged by which Hartley gave up his bedroom to the three Misses Trimblett and retired to a tiny room under the tiles. Miss Trimblett pointed out that it commanded a fine view.

"It is the only thing to be done," said Joan, softly.

"It isn't very big for three," said Miss Trimblett, referring to her own room, "but the twins won't be separated. I've always been used to a room to myself, but I suppose it can't be helped for the present."

She went downstairs and walked into the garden. The other members of the family were already there, and Hartley, watching them from the dining-room window, raised his brows in anguish as he noticed the partiality of the twins for cut flowers.

It was, as he soon discovered, one of the smallest of the troubles that followed on his sudden increase of family. His taste in easy-chairs met with the warm approval of George Trimblett, and it was clear that the latter regarded the tobacco-jar as common property. The twins' belongings—a joint-stock affair—occupied the most unlikely places in the house; and their quarrels were only exceeded in offensiveness by their noisy and uncouth endearments afterwards. Painstaking but hopeless attempts on the part of Miss Trimblett to "teach Rosa her place" added to the general confusion.

By the end of a month the Trimblett children were in full possession. George Trimblett, owing to the good offices of Mr. Vyner, senior, had obtained a berth in a shipping firm, but the others spent the days at home, the parties most concerned being unanimously of the opinion that it would be absurd to go to school before Christmas. They spoke with great fluency and good feeling of making a fresh start in the New Year.

"Interesting children," said Robert Vyner, who had dropped in one afternoon on the pretext of seeing how they were getting on. "I wish they were mine. I should be so proud of them."

Miss Hartley, who was about to offer him some tea, thought better of it, and, leaning back in her chair, regarded him suspiciously.

"And, after all, what is a garden for?" pursued Mr. Vyner, as a steady succession of thuds sounded outside, and Ted, hotly pursued by the twins, appeared abruptly in the front garden and dribbled a football across the flower-beds.

"They are spoiling the garden," said Joan, flushing. "Father is in despair."

Mr. Vyner shook his head indulgently. "Girls will be girls," he said, glancing through the window at Gertrude, who had thrown herself on the ball and was being dragged round the garden by her heels. "I'm afraid you spoil them, though."

Miss Hartley did not trouble to reply.

"I saw your eldest boy yesterday, at Marling's," continued the industrious Mr. Vyner. "He is getting on pretty well; Marling tells me he is steady and quiet. I should think that he might be a great comfort to you in your old age."

In spite of the utmost efforts to prevent it, Miss Hartley began to laugh. Mr. Vyner regarded her in pained astonishment.

"I didn't intend to be humorous," he said, with some severity. "I am fond of children, and, unfortunately, I—I am childless."

He buried his face in his handkerchief, and, removing it after a decent interval, found that his indignant hostess was preparing to quit the room.

"Don't go," he said, hastily. "I haven't finished yet."

"I haven't got time to stay and talk nonsense," said Joan.

"I'm not going to," said Robert, "but I want to speak to you. I have a confession to make."

"Confession?"

Mr. Vyner nodded with sad acquiescence. "I deceived you grossly the other day," he said, "and it has been worrying me ever since."

"It doesn't matter," said Joan, with a lively suspicion of his meaning.

"Pardon me," said Mr. Vyner, with solemn politeness, "if I say that it does. I—I lied to you, and I have been miserable ever since."

Joan waited in indignant silence.

"I told you that I was married," said Mr. Vyner, in thrilling tones. "I am not."

Miss Hartley, who had seated herself, rose suddenly with a fair show of temper. "You said you were not going to talk nonsense!" she exclaimed.

"I am not," said the other, in surprise. "I am owning to a fault, making a clean breast of my sins, not without a faint hope that I am setting an example that will be beautifully and bountifully followed."

"I have really got too much to do to stay here listening to nonsense," said Miss Hartley, vigorously.

"I am a proud man," resumed Mr. Vyner, "and what it has cost me to make this confession tongue cannot tell; but it is made, and I now, in perfect confidence—almost perfect confidence—await yours."

"I don't understand you," said Joan, pausing, with her hand on the door.

"Having repudiated my dear wife," said Mr. Vyner, sternly, "I now ask, nay, demand, that you repudiate Captain Trimblett—and all his works," he added, as ear-splitting screams sounded from outside.

"I wish—" began Joan, in a low voice.

"Yes?" said Robert, tenderly.

"That you would go."

Mr. Vyner started, and half rose to his feet. Then he thought better of it.

"I thought at first that you meant it," he said, with a slight laugh.

"I do mean it," said Joan, breathing quickly.

Robert rose at once. "I am very sorry," he said, with grave concern. "I did not think that you were taking my foolishness seriously."

"I ought to be amused, I know," said Joan, bitterly. "I ought to be humbly grateful to your father for having those children sent here. I ought to be flattered to think that he should remember my existence and make plans for my future."

"He—he believes that you are married to Captain Trimblett," said Robert.

"Fortunately for us," said Joan, dryly.

"Do you mean," said Robert, regarding her fixedly, "that my father arranged that marriage?"

Joan bit her lip. "No," she said at last.

"He had something to do with it," persisted Robert. "What was it?"

Joan shook her head.

"Well, I'll ask him about it," said Mr. Vyner.

"Please don't," said the girl. "It is my business."

"You have said so much," said Robert, "that you had better say more. That's what comes of losing your temper. Sit down and tell me all about it, please."

Joan shook her head again.

"You are not angry with me?" said Mr. Vyner.

"No."

"That's all right, then," said Robert, cheerfully. "That encourages me to go to still further lengths. You've got to tell me all about it. I forgot to tell you, but I'm a real partner in the firm now. I've got a hard and fast share in the profits—had it last Wednesday; since when I have already grown two inches. In exchange for this confidence I await yours. You must speak a little louder if you want me to hear."

"I didn't say anything," said the girl.

"You are wasting time, then," said Robert, shaking his head. "And that eldest girl of yours may come in at any moment."

Despite her utmost efforts Miss Hartley failed to repress a smile; greatly encouraged, Mr. Vyner placed a chair for her and took one by her side.

"Tell me everything, and I shall know where we are," he said, in a low voice.

"I would rather—" began Miss Hartley.

"Yes, I know," interrupted Mr. Vyner, with great gravity; "but we were not put into this world to please ourselves. Try again."

Miss Hartley endeavoured to turn the conversation, but in vain. In less than ten minutes, with a little skilful prompting, she had told him all.

"I didn't think that it was quite so bad as that," said Robert, going very red. "I am very sorry—very. I can't think what my father was about, and I suppose, in the first place, that it was my fault."

"Yours?" exclaimed Joan.

"For not displaying more patience," said Robert, slowly. "But I was afraid of—of being forestalled."

Miss Hartley succeeded in divesting her face of every atom of expression. Robert Vyner gazed at her admiringly.

"I am glad that you understand me," he murmured. "It makes things easier for me. I don't suppose that you have the faintest idea how shy and sensitive I really am."

Miss Hartley, without even troubling to look at him, said that she was quite sure she had not.

"Nobody has," said Robert, shaking his head, "but I am going to make a fight against it. I am going to begin now. In the first place I want you not to think too hardly of my father. He has been a very good father to me. We have never had a really nasty word in our lives."

"I hope you never will have," said Joan, with some significance.

"I hope not," said Robert; "but in any case I want to tell you—"

Miss Hartley snatched away the hand he had taken, and with a hasty glance at the door retreated a pace or two from him.

"What is the matter?" he inquired, in a low voice.

Miss Hartley's eyes sparkled.

"My eldest daughter has just come in," she said, demurely. "I think you had better go."

CHAPTER XXIII

Mrs. Chinnery received the news of her brother's marriage with a calmness that was a source of considerable disappointment and annoyance to her friends and neighbours. To begin with, nobody knew how it had reached her, and several worthy souls who had hastened to her, hot-foot, with what they had fondly deemed to be exclusive information had some difficulty in repressing their annoyance. Their astonishment was increased a week later on learning that she had taken a year's lease of No. 9, Tranquil Vale, which had just become vacant, and several men had to lie awake half the night listening to conjectures as to where she had got the money.

Most of the furniture at No. 5 was her own, and she moved it in piecemeal. Captain Sellers, who had his own ideas as to why she was coming to live next door to him, and was somewhat flattered in consequence, volunteered to assist, and, being debarred by deafness from learning that his services were refused, caused intense excitement by getting wedged under a dressing-table on the stairs.

To inquiries as to how he got there, the captain gave but brief replies, and those of an extremely sailorly description, the whole of his really remarkable powers being devoted for the time being to the question of how he was to get out. He was released at length by a man and a saw, and Mrs. Chinnery, as soon as she could speak, gave him a pressing invitation to take home with him any particular piece of the table for which he might have a fancy.

He was back next morning with a glue-pot, and divided his time between boiling it up on the kitchen stove and wandering about the house in search of things to stick. Its unaccountable disappearance during his absence in another room did much to mar the harmony of an otherwise perfect day. First of all he searched the house from top to bottom; then, screwing up his features, he beckoned quietly to Mrs. Chinnery.

"I hadn't left it ten seconds," he said, mysteriously. "I went into the front room for a bit of stick, and when I went back it had gone—vanished. I was never more surprised in my life."

"Don't bother me," said Mrs. Chinnery. "I've got enough to do."

"Eh?"

Mrs. Chinnery, who was hot and flustered, shook her head at him.

"It's a very odd thing," said Captain Sellers, shaking his head. "I never lost a glue-pot before in my life—never. Do you know anything about that charwoman that's helping you?"

"Yes, of course," said Mrs. Chinnery.

The captain put his hand to his ear.

"Yes, of course."

"I don't like her expression," said Captain Sellers, firmly. "I'm a very good judge of faces, and there's a look, an artful look, about her eyes that I don't like. It's my belief she's got my glue-pot stowed about her somewhere; and I'm going to search her."

"You get out of my house," cried the overwrought Mrs. Chinnery.

"Not without my glue-pot," said Captain Sellers, hearing for once. "Take that woman upstairs and search her. A glue-pot—a hot glue-pot—can't go without hands."

Frail in body but indomitable in spirit he confronted the accused, who, having overheard his remarks, came in and shook her fist in his face and threatened him with the terrors of the law.

"A glue-pot can't go without hands," he said, obstinately. "If you had asked me for a little you could have had it, and welcome; but you had no business to take it."

"Take it!" vociferated the accused. "What good do you think it would be to me? I've 'ad eleven children and two husbands, and I've never been accused of stealing a glue-pot before. Where do you think I could put it?"

"I don't know." said the captain, as soon as he understood. "That's what I'm curious about. You go upstairs with Mrs. Chinnery, and if she don't find that you've got that glue-pot concealed on you, I shall be very much surprised. Why not own up the truth before you scald yourself?"

Instead of going upstairs the charwoman went to the back door and sat on the step to get her breath, and, giving way to a sense of humour which had survived the two husbands and eleven children, wound up with a strong fit of hysterics. Captain Sellers, who watched through the window as she was being taken away, said that perhaps it was his fault for putting temptation in her way.

Mrs. Chinnery tried to keep her door fast next morning, but it was of no use. The captain was in and out all day, and, having found a tin of green paint and a brush among his stores, required constant watching. The day after Mrs. Chinnery saw her only means of escape, and at nine o'clock in the morning, with fair words and kind smiles, sent him into Salthaven for some picture-cord. He made four journeys that day. He came back from the last in a butcher's cart, and having handed Mrs. Chinnery the packet of hooks and eyes, for which he had taken a month's wear out of his right leg, bade her a hurried good-night and left for home on the arm of the butcher.

He spent the next day or two in an easy-chair by the fire, but the arrival of Mrs. Willett to complete the furnishing of No. 5 from her own surplus stock put him on his legs again. As an old neighbour and intimate friend of Mr. Truefitt's he proffered his services, and Mrs. Willett, who had an old-fashioned belief in "man," accepted them. His one idea—the pot of paint being to him like a penny in a schoolboy's pocket—was to touch things up a bit; Mrs. Willett's idea was for him to help hang pictures and curtains.

"The steps are so rickety they are only fit for a man," she screamed in his ear. "Martha has been over with them twice already."

Captain Sellers again referred to the touching-up properties of green paint. Mrs. Willett took it from him, apparently for the purpose of inspection, and he at once set out in search of the glue-pot.

"We'll do the curtains downstairs first," she said to Martha. "Upstairs can wait."

The captain spent the morning on the steps, his difficulties being by no means lessened by the tremolo movement which Martha called steadying them. Twice he was nearly shaken from his perch like an over-ripe plum, but all went well until they were hanging the curtains in the best bed-room, when Martha, stooping to recover a dropped ring, shut the steps up like a pair of compasses.

The captain, who had hold of the curtains at the time, brought them down with him, and lay groaning on the floor. With the help of her mistress, who came hurrying up on hearing the fall, Martha got him on to the bed and sent for the doctor.

"How do you feel?" inquired Mrs. Willett, eying him anxiously.

"Bad," said the captain, closing his eyes. "Every bone in my body is broken, I believe. It feels like it."

Mrs. Willett shook her head and sought for words to reassure him. "Keep your spirits up," she said, encouragingly. "Don't forget that: 'There's a sweet little cherub that sits up aloft to look after the life of poor Jack.'"

Captain Sellers opened his eyes and regarded her fixedly. "He wouldn't ha' been sitting there long if that fool Martha had been holding the steps," he said, with extraordinary bitterness.

He closed his eyes again and refused to speak until the doctor came. Then, having been stripped and put to bed for purposes of examination, he volunteered information as to his condition which twice caused the doctor to call him to order.

"You ought to be thankful it's no worse," he said, severely.

The captain sniffed. "When you've done pinching my leg," he said, disagreeably, "I'll put it back into bed again."

The doctor relinquished it at once, and, standing by the bed, regarded him thoughtfully.

"Well, you've had a shock," he said at last, "and you had better stay in bed for a few days."

"Not here," said Mrs. Willett, quickly. "My daughter and her husband will be home in a day or two."

The doctor looked thoughtful again; then he bent and spoke in the captain's ear.

"We are going to move you to your own house," he said.

"No, you're not," said the other, promptly.

"You'll be more comfortable there," urged the doctor.

"I'm not going to be moved," said Captain Sellers, firmly. "It might be fatal. I had a chap once—fell from aloft—and after he'd been in the saloon for a day or two I had him carried for'ard, and he died on the way. And he wasn't nearly as bad as I am."

"Well, we'll see how you are to-morrow," said the doctor, with a glance at Mrs. Willett.

"I shall be worse to-morrow," said the captain, cheerfully. "But I don't want to give any trouble. Send my housekeeper in to look after me. She can sleep in the next room."

They argued with him until his growing deafness rendered argument useless. A certain love of change and excitement would not be denied. Captain Sellers, attended by his faithful housekeeper, slept that night at No. 5, and awoke next morning to find his prognostications as to his condition fully confirmed.

"I'm aching all over," he said to Mrs. Willett. "I can't bear to be touched."

"You'll have to be moved to your own house," said Mrs. Chinnery, who had come in at Mrs. Willett's request to see what could be done. "We expect my brother home in a day or two."

"Let him come," said the captain, feebly. "I sha'n't bite him."

"But you're in his bed," said Mrs. Chinnery.

"Eh?"

"In his bed," screamed Mrs. Chinnery.

"I sha'n't bite him," repeated the captain.

"But he can't sleep with you," said Mrs. Chinnery, red with loud speaking.

"I don't want him to," said Captain Sellers. "I've got nothing against him, and, in a general way of speaking, I'm not what could be called a particular man—but I draw the line."

Mrs. Chinnery went downstairs hastily and held a council of war with Mrs. Willett and Martha. It was decided to wait for the doctor, but the latter, when he came, could give no assistance.

"He's very sore and stiff," he said, thoughtfully, "but it's nothing serious. It's more vanity than anything else; he likes being made a fuss of and being a centre of attraction. He's as tough as leather, and the most difficult old man I have ever encountered."

"Is he quite right in his head?" demanded Mrs. Chinnery, hotly.

The doctor pondered. "He's a little bit childish, but his head will give more trouble to other people than to himself," he said at last. "Be as patient with him as you can, and if you can once persuade him to get up, perhaps he will consent to be moved."

Mrs. Chinnery, despite a naturally hot temper, did her best, but in vain. Mrs. Willett was promptly denounced as a "murderess," and the captain, holding forth to one or two callers, was moved almost to tears as he reflected upon the ingratitude and hardness of woman. An account of the accident in the Salthaven Gazette, which described him as "lying at death's door," was not without its effect in confining him to Mr. Truefitt's bed.

The latter gentleman and his wife, in blissful ignorance of the accident, returned home on the following evening. Mrs. Willett and Mrs. Chinnery, apprised by letter, were both there to receive them, and the former, after keeping up appearances in a stately fashion for a few minutes, was finally persuaded to relent and forgive them both. After which, Mrs. Truefitt was about to proceed upstairs to take off her things, when she was stopped by Mrs. Chinnery.

"There—there is somebody in your room," said the latter.

"In my room?" said Mrs. Truefitt, in a startled voice.

"We couldn't write to you," said Mrs. Willett, with a little shade of reproach in her voice, "because you didn't give us your address. Captain Sellers had an accident and is in your bed."

"Who?" said the astounded Mr. Truefitt. "What!"

Mrs. Willett, helped by Mrs. Chinnery, explained the affair to him; Mr. Truefitt, with the exception of a few startled ejaculations, listened in sombre silence.

"Well, we must use the next room for to-night," he said at last, "and I'll have him out first thing in the morning."

"His housekeeper sleeps there," said Mrs. Willett, shaking her head.

"And a niece of hers, who helps her with him, in the little room," added Mrs. Chinnery.

Mr. Truefitt got up and walked about the room. Broken remarks about "a nice home-coming" and "galvanized mummies" escaped him at intervals. Mrs. Willett endured it for ten minutes, and then, suddenly remembering what was due to a mother-in-law, made a successful intervention. In a somewhat subdued mood they sat down to supper.

The Truefitts slept at Mrs. Willett's that night, but Mr. Truefitt was back first thing next morning to take possession of his own house. He found Captain Sellers, propped up with pillows, eating his breakfast, and more than dubious as to any prospects of an early removal.

"Better wait a week or two and see how I go on," he said, slowly. "I sha'n't give any trouble."

"But you are giving trouble," shouted the fuming Mr. Truefitt. "You're an absolute nuisance. If it hadn't been for your officiousness it wouldn't have happened."

The captain put his plate aside and drew himself up in the bed.

"Get out of my room," he said, in a high, thin voice.

"You get out of my bed," shouted the incensed Mr. Truefitt. "I'll give you ten minutes to dress yourself and get out of my house. If you're not out by then, I'll carry you out."

He waited downstairs for a quarter of an hour, and then, going to the bed-room again, discovered that the door was locked. Through the keyhole the housekeeper informed him that it was the captain's orders, and begged him to go away as the latter was now having his "morning's nap."

Captain Sellers left with flags flying and drums beating three days later. To friends and neighbours generally he confided the interesting fact that his departure was hastened by a nightly recurring dream of being bitten by sharks.

CHAPTER XXIV

The news that Mrs. Chinnery had taken a house of her own and was anxious to let rooms, gave Robert Vyner an idea which kept him busy the whole of an evening. First of all he broached it to Hartley, but finding him divided between joy and nervousness he took the matter into his own hands and paid a visit to Tranquil Vale; the result of which he communicated with some pride to Joan Hartley the same afternoon.

"It was my own idea entirely," he said with a feeble attempt to conceal a little natural pride. "Some people would call it an inspiration. Directly I heard that Mrs. Chinnery was anxious to let rooms I thought of your children—I mentioned the idea to your father and escaped an embrace by a hair's breadth. I was prepared to remind him that 'Absence makes the heart grow fonder' and to follow it up with 'Distance lends enchantment to the view'; but it was unnecessary. It will be a great thing for Mrs. Chinnery."

Miss Hartley looked thoughtful.

"And you," said Robert reproachfully.

"If father is satisfied—" began Miss Hartley.

"'Satisfied' is a cold and inadequate word," said Robert. "He was delighted. He could not have been more pleased if I had told him that the entire five had succumbed to an attack of croup. I left my work to look after itself to come and give you the news."

"You are very kind," said Joan, after some consideration.

"It is a good thing for all concerned," said Robert. "It is a load off my mind. The last time I was here, I was interrupted at a most critical moment by the entrance of Miss Trimblett."

"And now, instead of coming here to see them, you will have to go to Mrs. Chinnery's," said Joan.

"When I want to," said Mr. Vyner with a forced smile, as the twins came rushing into the room. "Yes."

The exodus took place three days afterward to the entire satisfaction of all concerned. Tranquil Vale alone regarded the advent of the newcomers with a certain amount of uneasiness, the joy of Ted and the twins when they found that there was a river at the bottom of the garden, threatening to pass all bounds. In a state of wild excitement they sat on the fence and waved to passing craft, until in an attempt to do justice to a larger ship than usual, Miss Gertrude Trimblett waved herself off the fence on to the stones of the foreshore below.

Captain Sellers, who had been looking on with much interest, at once descended and rendered first aid. It was the first case he had had since he had left the sea, but, after a careful examination, he was able to assure the sufferer that she had broken her right leg in two places. The discovery was received with howls of lamentation from both girls, until Dolly blinded with tears, happened to fall over the injured limb and received in return such hearty kicks from it that the captain was compelled to reconsider his diagnosis, and after a further examination discovered that it was only bent. In quite a professional manner he used a few technical terms that completely covered his discomfiture.

It was the beginning of a friendship which Tranquil Vale did its best to endure with fortitude, and against which Mrs. Chinnery fought in vain. In the company of Ted and the twins Captain Sellers renewed his youth. Together they discovered the muddiest places on the foreshore, and together they borrowed a neighbour's boat and sailed down the river in quest of adventures. With youth at the prow and dim-sighted age at the helm, they found several. News of their doings made Hartley congratulate himself warmly on their departure.

"Mrs. Chinnery is just the woman to manage them," he said to Joan, "and Truefitt tells me that having children to look after has changed her wonderfully."

Miss Hartley, with a little shiver, said she could quite understand it.

"I mean for the better," said her father, "he said she is getting quite young and jolly again. And he told me that young Saunders is there a great deal." Miss Hartley raised her eyebrows in mute interrogation.

"He pretends that he goes to see George," said her father, dropping his voice, "but Truefitt thinks that it is Jessie. I suppose Trimblett won't mind; he always thought a lot of Saunders. I don't know whether you ought to interfere."

"Certainly not," said Joan flushing. "What has it got to do with me?"

"Well, I just mentioned it," said Hartley, "although I suppose Mrs. Chinnery is mostly responsible while they are with her. I am writing to tell Trimblett that the children are at Tranquil Vale. When he comes back perhaps, he will make other arrangements."

"Very likely," said his daughter abruptly, "or perhaps he will marry Mrs. Chinnery."

Mr. Hartley, who was at supper, put down his knife and fork and sat eying her in very natural amazement. "Marry Mrs. Chinnery?" he gasped, "but how can he?"

"I mean," said Joan with a sudden remembrance of the state of affairs, "I mean if anything should happen to me."

Mr. Hartley finished his supper and drawing his chair up to the fire sat smoking in thoughtful silence.

"And if anything happens to Trimblett perhaps you will marry again," he said at last.

Miss Hartley shook her head. "I am not afraid," she said ambiguously.

Her confidence was put to the test less than a fortnight later by an unexpected visit from Mr. Robert Vyner, who, entering the room in a somewhat breathless condition, accepted a chair and sat gazing at her with an air of mysterious triumph.

"I'm the bearer of important news," he announced. "Dispatches from the front. You'll hear all about it from your father when he comes home, but I wanted to be the first with it."

"What is the matter?" inquired Joan.

Mr. Vyner looked shocked. "All important news, good or bad, should be broken gently," he said reproachfully. "Do you know any Scotch?"

"Scotch!" said the mystified Miss Hartley.

Mr. Vyner nodded. "The best laid schemes o' mice and men gang oft agley," he quoted in a thrilling voice. "Do you understand that?"

"I'll wait till father comes home," announced Miss Hartley, with some decision.

"There are other quotations bearing on the matter in hand," said Mr. Vyner, thoughtfully, "but I have forgotten them. At present I am thinking of you to the utter exclusion of everything else. Not that that is anything unusual. Far from it. To cut a long story short, Captain Trimblett has been left behind at San Francisco with malaria, and the mate has taken the ship on."

Miss Hartley gave a little cry of concern.

"He has had it before," said Mr. Vyner composedly, "but he seems to have got it bad this time, and when he is fit enough, he is coming home. Now what are you going to do?"

"Poor Captain Trimblett," said Joan. "I am so sorry."

"What are you going to do?" repeated Mr. Vyner, impressively. "His children are at Salthaven, and he will live here because my father and I had practically decided to give him the berth of ship's husband after this voyage. He will have it a little sooner, that's all. Appropriate berth for a marrying man like that, isn't it? Sounds much more romantic than marine superintendent."

"I made sure that he would be away for at least two years," said Joan, regarding him helplessly.

"There is nothing certain in this world," said Mr. Vyner, sedately. "You should have thought of that before. The whole thing is bound to come out now. There are only two courses open to you. You might marry Captain Trimblett in reality—"

"What is the other?" inquired Joan, as he paused.

"The other," said Mr. Vyner slowly and lowering his voice, "the other stands before you. All he can urge in his favour is, that he is younger than Trimblett, and, as I have said on another occasion, with—"

"If there is nothing more than that in his favour—" said Joan turning away.

"Nothing," said Robert, humbly, "unless—"

"Unless what?"

"Unless you know of anything."

Joan Hartley, her gaze still averted, shook her head.

"Still," said Mr. Vyner, with an air of great thoughtfulness, "a paragon would be awful to live with. Awful. Fancy marrying Bassett for instance! Fancy being married to a man you could never find fault with."

"There is a third course open to me," said Joan, turning round. "I could go away."

Mr. Vyner got up slowly and took a step toward her. "Would you—would you sooner go away than stay with me?" he said in a low voice.

"I—I don't want to go away," said Joan after a long pause.

Mr. Vyner took two more steps.

"I'm so fond of Salthaven," added Joan hastily.

"So am I," said Robert. "It seems to me that we have a lot of ideas in common. Don't you think it would simplify matters if you stayed at Salthaven and married me?"

Joan eyed him gravely. "I don't think it would simplify matters with your father," she said, slowly.

Mr. Vyner's fourth and last step took him to her chair.

"Is that your only objection?" he murmured, bending over her.

"I might think of others—in time," said Joan.

Mr. Vyner bent a little lower, but so slowly that Miss Hartley was compelled to notice it. She got up suddenly and confronted him. He took both her hands in his, but so gently that she offered no resistance.

"That is a bargain," he said, trying to steady his voice. "I will soon arrange matters with my father."

Joan smiled faintly and shook her head.

"You'll see," said Robert confidently. "I've been a good son to him, and he knows it. And I always have had my own way. I'm not going to alter now. It wouldn't be good for him."

"You are holding my hands," said Joan.

"I know," said Mr. Vyner. "I like it."

He released them reluctantly and stood looking at her. Miss Hartley after a brave attempt to meet his gaze, lowered her eyes. For a time neither of them spoke.

"I'm as bad as Trimblett," said Robert at last. "I am beginning to believe in fate. It is my firm opinion that we were intended for each other. I can't imagine marrying anybody else, can you?"

Miss Hartley, still looking down, made no reply.

CHAPTER XXV

Robert Vyner walked home slowly, trying as he went to evolve a scheme which should in the first place enable him to have his own way, and, in the second to cause as little trouble as possible to everybody. As a result of his deliberations he sought his father, whom he found enjoying a solitary cup of tea, and told him that he had been to Hartley's with the news of Captain Trimblett's illness. He added casually that Mrs. Trimblett was looking remarkably well. And he spoke feelingly of the pleasure afforded to all right-minded people at being able to carry a little sympathy and consolation into the homes of the afflicted.

Mr. Vyner senior sipped his tea. "She has got her father and the children if she wants sympathy," he said gruffly.

Robert shook his head. "It's not quite the same thing," he said gravely.

"The children ought to be with her," said his father. "I never understood why they should have gone to Mrs. Chinnery; still that's not my affair."

"It was to assist Mrs. Chinnery for one thing," said Robert. "And besides they were awfully in the way."

He heard his father put his tea-cup down and felt, rather than saw, that he was gazing at him with some intentness. With a pre-occupied air he rose and left the room.

Satisfied with the impression he had made, he paid another visit to Hartley's on the day following and then, despite Joan's protests, became an almost daily visitor. His assurance that they were duty visits paid only with a view to their future happiness only served to mystify her. The fact that Hartley twice plucked up courage to throw out hints as to the frequency of his visits, and the odd glances with which his father favoured him, satisfied him that he was in the right path.

For a fortnight he went his way unchecked, and, apparently blind to the growing stiffness, of his father every time the subject was mentioned, spoke freely of Mrs. Trimblett and the beautiful resignation with which she endured her husband's misfortunes. His father listened for the most part in silence, until coming at last to the conclusion, that there was nothing to be gained by that policy he waited until his wife had left the dining-room one evening and ventured a solemn protest.

"She is a very nice girl," said the delighted Robert.

"Just so," said his father, leaning toward a candle and lighting his cigar, "although perhaps that is hardly the way to speak of a married woman."

"And we have been friends for a long time," said Robert.

Mr. Vyner coughed dryly.

"Just so," he said again.

"Why shouldn't I go and see her when I like?" said Robert, after a pause.

"She is another man's wife," said his father, "and it is a censorious world."

Robert Vyner looked down at the cloth. "If she were not, I suppose there would be some other objection?" he said gloomily.

Mr. Vyner laid his cigar on the side of a plate and drew himself up. "My boy," he said impressively, "I don't think I deserve that. Both your mother and myself would—ha—always put your happiness before our own private inclinations."

He picked up his cigar again and placing it in his mouth looked the personification of injured fatherhood.

"Do you mean," said Robert, slowly, "do you mean that if she were single you would be willing for me to marry her?"

"It is no good discussing that," said Mr. Vyner with an air of great consideration.

"But would you?" persisted his son.

Mr. Vyner was a very truthful man as a rule, but there had been instances—he added another.

"Yes," he said with a slight gasp.

Robert sprang up with a haste that overturned his coffee, and seizing his father's hand shook it with enthusiasm. Mr. Vyner somewhat affected, responded heartily.

"Anything possible for you, Bob," he said, fervently, "but this is impossible."

His son looked at him. "I have never known you to go back on your word," he said emphatically.

"I never have," said Mr. Vyner.

"Your word is your bond," said Robert smiling at him. "And now I want to tell you something."

"Well," said the other, regarding him with a little uneasiness.

"She is not married," said Robert, calmly.

Mr. Vyner started up and his cigar fell unheeded to the floor.

"What!" he said, loudly.

"She is not married," repeated his son.

Mr. Vyner sank back in his chair again and looking round mechanically for his cigar, found it tracing a design on the carpet.

"Damn," he said fervently, as he stooped to remove it. He tossed it in his plate and leaning back glared at his son.

"Do you mean that she didn't marry Trimblett?" he inquired in a trembling voice.

"Yes."

Mr. Vyner drew the cigar-box toward him and selecting a cigar with great care, nipped off the end and, having lighted it, sat smoking in silence.

"This is very extraordinary," he said at last watching his son's eyes.

"I suppose she had a reason," said Robert in a matter-of-fact voice.

Mr. Vyner winced. He began to realize the state of affairs and sat trembling in impotent. Then he rose and paced up and down. He thought of his veiled threats to Hartley, the idea that his son should know of them added his anger.

"You are of full age," he said bitterly, "and have your own income—now."

Robert flushed and then turned pale.

"I will give that up if you wish, provided you'll retain Hartley," he said, quietly.

Mr. Vyner continued his perambulation smoked furiously and muttered something "forcing conditions upon him."

"I can't leave Hartley in the lurch," said he quietly. "It's not his fault. I can look to myself."

Mr. Vyner stopped and regarded him. "Don't be a fool," he said, shortly. "If it wasn't for mother—"

His son repressed a smile by an effort and feel more at ease. One of Mrs. Vyner's privileges was to serve as an excuse for any display of weakness of which her husband might be guilty.

"This pretended marriage will be a further scandal," said Mr. Vyner, frowning. "What are you going to tell people?"

"Nothing," said Robert.

"Do you think it is conducive to discipline to marry the daughter of my chief clerk?" continued his father.

Robert shook his head.

"No," he said, decidedly. "I have been thinking of that. It would be better to give him a small interest in the firm—equal to his salary, say."

Well aware of the uses of physical exercise at moments of mental stress, Mr. Vyner started on his walk again. He began to wonder whether, after all, he ought to consider his wife's feelings in the matter.

"She is a very nice girl," said Robert, after watching him for some time. "I wish you knew her."

Mr. Vyner waved the remark away with a large impatient hand.

"She declines to marry me against your wishes," continued his son, "but now that you have given your consent—"

The room suddenly became too small for Mr. Vyner. He passed out into the hall and a few seconds later his son heard the library door close with an eloquent bang. He shrugged his shoulders and lighting a cigarette sat down to wait. He was half-way through his third cigarette when the door opened and his father came into the room again.

"I have been talking to your mother," said Mr. Vyner, in a stately fashion. "She is very much upset, of course. Very. She is not strong, and I—ha—we came to the conclusion that you must do as you please."

He stepped to the table and with a trembling hand helped himself to a whiskey and soda. Robert took up a glass with a little claret in it.

"Success to the young couple," he said cheerfully.

Mr. Vyner paused with the glass at his lips and eyed him indignantly. Then with a wooden expression of face—intended possibly to suggest that he had not heard—took a refreshing drink. He placed the glass on the table and turned to see his son's outstretched hand.

CHAPTER XXVI

Captain Trimblett was back again in his old quarters, and already so much improved in health that he was able to repel with considerable vigor the many inquirers who were anxious to be put in possession of the real facts concerning his pretended marriage. It was a subject on which the captain was dumb, but in some mysterious fashion it came to be understood that it was a device on the part of a self-sacrificing and chivalrous ship-master to save Miss Hartley from the attentions of a determined admirer she had met in London. It was the version sanctioned—if not invented—by Mr. Robert Vyner.

It was a source of some little protestation of spirit to Miss Jelks that the captain had been brought home by his faithful boatswain. Conduct based on an idea of two years' absence had to be suddenly and entirely altered. She had had a glimpse of them both on the day of their arrival, but the fact that Mr. Walters was with his superior officer, and that she was with Mr. Filer, prevented her from greeting him.

In the wrath of his dismissal Mr. Filer met him more than half-way.

"Somebody 'ad to look arter 'im," said Mr. Walters, referring to the captain, as he sat in Rosa's kitchen the following evening, "and he always 'ad a liking for me. Besides which I wanted to get 'ome and see you."

"You have got it bad," said Rosa with a gratified titter.

"Look arter you, I ought to ha' said," retorted Mr. Walters, glowering at her, "and from wot I hear from Bassett, it's about time I did."

"Ho!" said Miss Jelks, taking a deep breath. "Ho, really!"

"I had it out of 'im this morning," continued Mr. Walters, eying her sternly; "I waited for 'im as he come out of his 'ouse. He didn't want to tell me at first, but when he found as 'ow he'd been late for the office if he didn't, he thought better of it."

Miss Jelks leaned back in her chair with a ladylike sneer upon her expressive features.

"I'll Bassett him," she said slowly.

"And I'll Filer him," said Mr. Walters, not to be outdone in the coining of verbs.

"It's a pity he don't say them things to my face," said Rosa, "I'd soon let him know."

"He's going to," said the boatswain readily. "I said we'd meet him on Sunday arternoon by Kegg's boat-house. Then we'll see wot you've got to say for yourself. Shut that door D'ye want to freeze me!"

"I'll shut it when you're gone," said Rosa calmly. "Make haste, else I shall catch cold. I'll go with you on Sunday afternoon—just so as you can beg my pardon—and after that I don't want anything more to do with you. You'd try the temper of a saint, you would."

Mr. Walters looked round the warm and comfortable kitchen, and his face fell. "I ain't going to judge you till I've heard both sides," he said slowly, and then seeing no signs of relenting in Rosa's face, passed out into the black night.

He walked down to the rendezvous on Sunday afternoon with a well-dressed circle. Miss Jelks only spoke to him once, and that was when he trod on her dress. A nipping wind stirred the surface of the river, and the place was deserted except for the small figure of Bassett sheltering under the lee of the boat-house. He came to meet them and raising a new bowler hat stood regarding Miss Jelks with an expression in which compassion and judicial severity were pretty evenly combined.

"Tell me, afore her, wot you told me the other day," said Mr. Walters, plunging at once into business.

"I would rather not," said Bassett, adjusting his spectacles and looking from one to the other, "but in pursuance of my promise, I have no alternative."

"Fire away," commanded the boatswain.

Bassett coughed, and then in a thin but firm voice complied. The list of Miss Jelks's misdeeds was a long one, and the day was cold, but he did not miss a single item. Miss Jelks, eying him with some concern as he proceeded, began to think he must have eyes at the back of his head. The boatswain, whose colour was deepening as he listened, regarded her with a lurid eye.

"And you believe it all," said Rosa, turning to him with a pitying smile as Bassett concluded his tale. "Why don't he go on; he ain't finished yet."

"Wot!" said Mr. Walters with energy.

"He ain't told you about making love to me yet," said Rosa.

"I didn't," said the youth. "I shouldn't think of doing such a thing. It was all a mistake of yours."

Miss Jelks uttered a cruel laugh. "Ask him whether he followed me like a pet dog," she said turning to the astonished boatswain. "Ask him if he didn't say he loved the ground my feet trod on. Ask him if he wanted to take me to Marsham Fair and cried because I wouldn't go."

"Eh?" gasped the boatswain, staring at the bewildered Bassett

"Ask him if he didn't go down on his knees to me in Pringle's Lane one day—a muddy day—and ask me to be his," continued the unscrupulous Rosa. "Ask him if he didn't say I was throwing myself away on a wooden-headed boatswain with bandy legs."

"Bandy wot?" ejaculated the choking Mr. Walters, as he bestowed an involuntary glower at the limbs in question.

"I can assure you I never said so," said Bassett; earnestly. "I never noticed before that they were bandy. And I never—"

An enormous fist held just beneath his nose stopped him in mad career.

"If you was only three foot taller and six or seven stone 'eavier," said the palpitating boatswain, "I should know wot to do with you.

"I assure you—" began Bassett.

"If you say another word," declared Mr. Walters, in grating accents, "I'll take you by the scruff of your little neck and drop you in the river. And if you tell any more lies about my young woman to a living soul I'll tear you limb from limb, and box your ears arter-wards."

With a warning shake of the head at the gasping Bassett he turned to Miss Jelks, but that injured lady, with her head at an alarming angle, was already moving away. Even when he reached her side she seemed unaware of his existence, and it was not until the afternoon was well advanced that she deigned to take the slightest notice of his abject apologies.

"It's being at sea and away from you that does it," he said humbly.

"And a nasty jealous temper," added Miss Jelks.

"I'm going to try for a shore-berth," said her admirer. "I spoke to Mr. Vyner—the young one—about it yesterday, and he's going to see wot he can do for me. If I get that I shall be a different man."

"He'd do anything for Miss Joan," said the mollified Rosa thoughtfully, "and if you behave yourself and conquer your wicked jealous nature I might put in a word for you with her myself."

Mr. Walters thanked her warmly and with a natural anxiety regarding his future prospects, paid frequent visits to learn what progress she was making. He haunted the kitchen with the persistency of a blackbeetle, and became such a nuisance at last that Miss Hartley espoused his cause almost with enthusiasm.

"He is very much attached to Rosa, but he takes up a lot of her time," she said to Robert Vyner as they were on their way one evening to Tranquil Vale to pay a visit to Captain Trimblett.

"I'll get him something for Rosa's sake," said Robert, softly. "I shall never forget that she invited me to breakfast when her mistress would have let me go empty away. Do you remember?"

"I remember wondering whether you were going to stay all day," said Joan.

"It never occurred to me," said Mr. Vyner in tones of regret. "I'm afraid you must have thought me very neglectful."

They walked on happily through the dark, cold night until the lighted windows of Tranquil Vale showed softly in the blackness. There was a light in the front room of No. 5, and the sound of somebody moving hurriedly about followed immediately upon Mr. Vyner's knock. Then the door opened and Captain Trimblett stood before them.

"Come in," he said heartily. "Come in, I'm all alone this evening."

He closed the door behind them, and, while Mr. Vyner stood gazing moodily at the mound on the table which appeared to have been hastily covered up with a rather soiled towel, placed a couple of easy chairs by the fire. Mr. Vyner, with his eyes still on the table, took his seat slowly, and then transferring his regards to Captain Trimblett, asked him in a stern vein what he was smiling at Joan for.

"She smiled at me first," said the captain.

Mr. Vyner shook his head at both of them, and at an offer of a glass of beer looked so undecided that the captain, after an uneasy glance at the table, which did not escape Mr. Vyner, went to the kitchen to procure some.

"I wonder," said Robert musingly, as he turned to the table, "I wonder if it would be bad manners to—"

"Yes," said Joan, promptly.

Mr. Vyner sighed and tried to peer under a corner of the towel. "I can see a saucer," he announced, excitedly.

Miss Hartley rose and pointing with a rigid fore-finger at her own chair, changed places with him.

"You want to see yourself," declared Mr. Vyner.

Miss Hartley scorned to reply.

"Let's share the guilt," continued the other. "You shut your eyes and raise the corner of the towel, and I'll do the 'peeping'."

The return of the unconscious captain with the beer rendered a reply unnecessary.

"We half thought you would be at number nine," he said as the captain poured him out a glass.

"I'm keeping house this evening," said the captain, "or else I should have been."

"It's nice for you to have your children near you," said Joan, softly.

Captain Trimblett assented. "And it's nice to be able to give up the sea," he said with a grateful glance at Vyner. "I'm getting old, and that last bout of malaria hasn't made me any younger."

"The youngsters seem to get on all right with Mrs. Chinnery," said Robert, eying him closely.

"Splendidly," said the Captain. "I should never have thought that she would have been so good with children. She half worships them."

"Not all of them," said Mr. Vyner.

"All of 'em," said the captain.

"Twins, as well?" said Mr. Vyner, raising his voice.

"She likes them best of all," was the reply.

Mr. Vyner rose slowly from his chair. "She is a woman in a million," he said impressively. "I wonder why—"

"They're very good girls," said the captain hastily. "Old Sellers thinks there is nobody like them."

"I expect you'll be making a home for them soon," said Robert, thoughtfully; "although it will be rather hard on Mrs. Chinnery to part with them. Won't it?"

"We are all in the hands of fate," said the captain gazing suddenly at his tumbler. "Fate rules all things from the cradle to the grave."

He poured himself out a little more beer and lapsing into a reminiscent mood cited various instances in his own career, in confirmation. It was an interesting subject, but time was pressing and Mr. Vyner, after a regretful allusion to that part, announced that they must be going. Joan rose, and Captain Trimblett, rising at the same moment, knocked over his beer and in a moment of forgetfulness snatched the towel from the table to wipe it up. The act revealed an electro-plated salad-bowl of noble proportions, a saucer of whitening and some pieces of rag.

W.W. Jacobs – A Short Biography

William Wymark Jacobs was born on September 8, 1863 in the Wapping district of London, England. An author, humorist and dramatist, Jacobs is best remembered for the enduring classic tale of horror - "The Monkey's Paw".

As a youth, Jacobs grew up near the Wapping docks in London, where his father was a wharf manager. The family's first home was home was a house on a River Thames wharf.

The docklands setting would show up frequently in his later literary output. Jacobs, the wharf rat, and his three siblings lost their mother when they were all still young children. Their father, William Gage Jacobs, remarried and fathered a further seven children with his erstwhile housekeeper Ellen Florey. Although he grew up surrounded by poverty, Jacobs himself received a formal education in London, first at a private prep school and later at the Birkbeck Literary and Scientific Institute (now part of the University of London and known as Birkbeck College).

Jacobs' adult working life began with a clerical position at the Post Office Savings Bank. The job was not a stimulating one but Jacobs put his imagination to good use and started to write short stories, sketches and articles, many of which appeared in the Post Office house publication "Blackfriars Magazine."

Although Jacobs did receive his fair share of rejection slips at the beginning of his career, many works written during this period of clerical employment appeared in the "Idler" and "Today" magazines, both of which were edited by noted humorist Jerome K. Jerome, who had taken a liking to Jacobs' stories.

From 1898, Jacobs also published stories in "The Strand", a popular, monthly fiction and general interest magazine. The arrangement stayed in place for most of his life and many of the works in

Jacobs' subsequent collections – including the nautical serialization A Master of Craft (1899-1900) - appeared there first.

Jacobs' first volume of collected works was published in 1896. Many Cargoes, a selection of sea-faring yarns, established Jacobs as a popular writer and humorist with a penchant for authentic dialogue and trick endings (critics of the day referred to him as the "O. Henry of the Waterfront").

A year later he published a novelette, The Skipper's Wooing, and in 1898 and another collection of short stories titled Sea Urchins. These works painted vivid, if imaginatively stretched, pictures of dockland and seafaring London with colourful characters (such as "The Night Watchman", Ginger Dick) that now seem archetypal.

Many of Jacobs' periodical publications and first editions were illustrated with woodcuts and ink drawings, as was still the custom at the turn of the 20th century. The author worked regularly with artists such as E.W. Kemble, who had illustrated Mark Twain's Adventures of Huckleberry Finn and Harriet Beecher Stowe's Uncle Tom's Cabin, and his good friend Will Owen, who eventually became a household name on the strength of his iconic Bisto Kids, Bovril and Lux Soap advertising posters.

By 1899, Jacobs was able to quit the post office and finally begin a career making a living as a full-time writer.

He married the noted suffragist Agnes Eleanor Williams (who had been jailed for her protest activities) in 1900. They set up a household in Loughton, Essex as well as living part of the year in central London. The couple went on to have five children together though their marriage was considered an unhappy one.

The publication of two short novels: At Sunwich Port (a romantic tale of rival sea captains in the fictional seaside community of Sunwich standing in for the actual East England community of Sandwich, Kent) and Dialstone Lane (another small town romance involving intrigue and buried treasure), in 1902 and 1904 respectively, cemented Jacobs' reputation as one of the leading British authors of the new century.

On the foundations of a continuing ability to write for his audience he was readily published though he never strayed too far from what was becoming his familiar, dependable style. There followed a string of further successful publications, including Captain's All (1905), Night Watches (1914), The Castaways (1916), and Sea Whispers (1926). Jacobs published eighteen books in all during his lifetime; thirteen collections and five novels.

As a storyteller, Jacobs is perhaps better remembered for a handful of brief tales of the supernatural than for his popular nautical-themed works. The most famous of these, The Monkey's Paw, originally appeared as part of the 1902 short story collection The Lady of the Barge. It is an economically written story about a shriveled talisman, a monkey's paw that brings grief and horror in the wake of all too literal wish granting. The story has been adapted for other media repeatedly, starting with a one-act play performed at London's Haymarket Theatre in 1903. There have been multiple film adaptations of the story in the modern era; some of us are familiar with its appearance in an episode of the popular animated series, The Simpsons.

Another macabre gem, The Toll-House, was published as part of the collection Sailor's Knots in 1909. Jacob's once again employs a sparse style to tell the story of a group of men who spend the night in a famously haunted house on a dare (a noticeably similar narrative concept was put to use in the much earlier play The Ghost of Jerry Bundler, which had launched Jacobs' parallel career as a dramatist back in 1899 when it was produced at the St. James Theatre in London). Innovative at the time of writing, these sparingly written, atmospheric ghost stories are now familiar classics of the supernatural genre.

Though prolific in his younger years, Jacobs' productivity dropped dramatically after the start of World War I. Yet even in self-imposed semi-retirement Jacobs was still recognized as a leading humorist, ranked alongside such writers as P. G. Wodehouse and George Birmingham. He enjoyed continuing influence and elevated status among his fellow writers as evidenced by these comments attributed to his colleague Henry James:

"Mr. Jacobs, I envy you. You are popular! Your admirable work is appreciated by a wide circle of readers; it has achieved popularity. Mine never goes into a second edition."

James' literary fortunes would, of course, change, but his back-handedly complimentary admiration is compelling evidence of Jacobs' reputation as a writer and humourist both for his audience and his perhaps more admired literary colleagues.

Though Jacobs would create little in the way of new work after 1911, he was still writing. In these later years, seemingly burnt out creatively, Jacobs concentrated more on writing dramatizations and adaptations of his existing stories, including Beauty and the Barge (a film version starring Margaret Rutherford was also released in 1937) and In the Dark (a one act play that is often performed pr published with The Monkey's Paw adaptation).

Though admired by loyal readers throughout his lifetime, Jacobs has been almost completely forgotten since. Critics are at a loss to name a single reason why - Jacobs is universally considered to be a fine and imaginative literary craftsman. But, as critic John Wain suggested in a 1960 essay, perhaps Jacobs' humour may have been too gentle to persist into the cruel and sarcastic modern era, his dry pokes at proletariat hardship no longer suiting the times.

Nonetheless, Jacobs' legacy remains solid: he continued Dickens' (a writer with whom he is also often compared) tradition for sharing working class stories in authentic vernacular. And polished narratives such as The Monkey's Paw set a standard for the clever use of horror in fiction and popular culture that endures to this day. Indeed recently his works have begun to show an increased demand and appreciation in a world that is constantly looking over its shoulder.

William Wymark Jacobs died in a North London nursing home in Hornsey Lane, Islington on September 1st, 1943, just a week before his 80th birthday.

W.W. Jacobs – A Concise Bibliography

NOVELS AND SHORT STORY COLLECTIONS
MANY CARGOES (SHORT STORIES) (1896)
THE SKIPPER'S WOOING (1897)
SEA URCHINS (SHORT STORIES) (1898) aka MORE CARGOES
A MASTER OF CRAFT (1900)
LIGHT FREIGHTS (SHORT STORIES) (1901)
THE LADY OF THE BARGE (SHORT STORIES) (1902)
AT SUNWICH PORT (1902)
DIALSTONE LANE (1902)

SALTHAVEN (1908)
CAPTAINS ALL (SHORT STORIES) (1911)
NIGHT WATCHERS (SHORT STORIES) (1914)
DEEP WATERS (SHORT STORIES) (1919)

MONEY CHANGERS
THE MONEY-BOX
THE MONKEY'S PAW
MRS. BUNKER'S CHAPERON
THE NEST EGG
ODD MAN OUT
THE OLD MAN OF THE SEA
OUTSAILED
OVER THE SIDE
PAYING OFF
THE PERSECUTION OF BOB PRETTY
PETER'S PENCE
PICKLED HERRING
PRIVATE CLOTHES
PRIZE MONEY
THE RESURRECTION OF MR. WIGGETT
THE RIVAL BEAUTIES
RULE OF THREE
SAM'S BOY
SAM'S GHOST
SELF-HELP
SENTENCE DEFERRED
SHAREHOLDERS
SKILLED ASSISTANCE
THE SKIPPER OF THE "OSPREY"
SMOKED SKIPPER
STEPPING BACKWARDS
STRIKING HARD
THE SUBSTITUTE
THE TEMPTATION OF SAMUEL BURGE
THE TEST
THE THREE SISTERS
TO HAVE AND TO HOLD
"THE TOLL-HOUSE"
TWIN SPIRITS
TWO OF A TRADE
THE UNDERSTUDY
THE UNKNOWN
THE VIGIL
WATCH-DOGS
THE WEAKER VESSEL
THE WELL
THE WHITE CAT

STAGE
THE GHOST OF JERRY BUNDLER (1899) (In London)

FILM ADAPTATIONS
A MASTER OF CRAFT (1922)

THE MONKEY'S PAW (1933)
OUR RELATIONS, a Laurel & Hardy film, "suggested by" to Jacobs' "The Money Box." (1936)
FOOTSTEPS IN THE FOG, from the short story The Interruption. (1955)

www.ingramcontent.com/pod-product-compliance
Lightning Source LLC
Chambersburg PA
CBHW071355170626

46811CB00003B/1136